the creek

KYLE LOCKHAVEN

For information about this title or to order other books and/or electronic media, contact the publisher:
Ashkad Publishing
P.O. Box 4572, West Richland, WA 99353
Ashkadpublishing@gmail.com

ISBN: 978-1-7322438-0-4

Printed in the United States of America

Cover and Interior design: 1106 Design

For every book sold, $1 will be donated to the Washington State Council of Fire Fighters Burn Foundation. (Whether it's a million or, far more likely, just the one that my mom buys.) They sponsor Camp Eyabsut, a free summer camp for burn survivors ages seven to seventeen. For more information, or to donate directly, go to campeyabsut.org

For Alicia
My first reader and the love of my life

Here is the world. Beautiful and terrible things will happen. Don't be afraid.

—Frederick Buechner

Chapter 1

THE INJURED, STARVING WOLF wasn't the most ominous thing threatening the two brothers, but it was the most immediate. As they carried on, blissfully unaware of its presence among the trees at the edge of the small meadow, the wolf was waiting for its chance.

The boys lay in the dirt near the creek watching two snails glide along a fallen branch. They were cheering for their chosen snail to win in a race.

The emaciated wolf emerged from the tree line. Crouching as low as its injured front leg would allow, it crept closer. Its approach was mostly concealed by the tall grass and wildflowers, although if the boys' attention had not been directed elsewhere, they'd have seen it coming. From the trees to where the boys were transfixed stretched about fifty feet of lush meadow that gently sloped down toward the creek. The wolf had made up half that distance when it stopped and lay down to reevaluate.

Meanwhile the cheering was building to a crescendo and the race was coming to an end. The smaller of the boys jumped up and threw his hands in the air, celebrating victory. The bigger of the two stood up and brushed off the dirt and pine needles from the front of his clothes. He gave his brother a high five, turned around, and made two very familiar jumps from the bank of the creek to the small island in the middle, then to the other bank.

The wolf saw its window of opportunity fling open. Abandoning the cover, it limped as fast as it could toward the smaller boy, who was jumping up and down with his back turned to the meadow. The distance between the two was nearly closed. It turned its head and exposed its menacing front teeth. It was just about to strike when a rock smashed to the ground in front of it and bounced up, striking it in the chest. The yell of a man possessed filled the meadow. The wolf yelped, causing the smaller boy to spin around. Another rock hit the ground just beside its bloody leg, followed by a third that struck it directly in the left eye.

Another cry of agony and the wolf turned and ran for the forest, ignoring the pain in its leg.

The man ran toward the small boy, jumped over the creek, and scooped him up. He stood and held the boy as he watched the wolf disappear into the trees. The bigger boy crossed the creek again and ran to the man. Holding the smaller boy in one arm, he reached out with the other to embrace the bigger boy. The three of them remained in the embrace for a long time.

Chapter 2

"WHAT WERE YOU DOING out here, Dad?" said the bigger boy, Caleb, after the moment had passed. He was tall and skinny, fourteen years old, with dark brown hair. His ears were just a little too big for his head.

After a brief pause Dad said, "Nothing, just getting you guys. It's time for dinner." The sky was barely beginning to darken on a warm summer night.

Caleb thought, *Why not just ring the dinner bell like usual?*

"I've never seen a wolf before," said Connor, the smaller boy. He had a little more meat on his bones than his older brother, but not much. His hair was a few shades lighter brown and his eyes were hazel. He was still visibly shaken as Dad set him back on the ground. "Was he gonna kill me?"

"I don't know, Connor, they usually try to avoid people." Dad looked back behind them as they headed toward home. "That one looked hurt and really skinny, though. You boys'll have to keep your heads on swivels when you're out here from now on."

"You saved my life," Connor said, trying to hold back tears. His efforts were in vain; he couldn't hold them back any longer and he broke down.

Dad picked him up in stride and carried him on his left hip like he was a two-year-old, not the eighty-pound eleven-year-old that he'd grown to be. Their dad was naturally skinny but had added some muscle to his frame during his time at the firehouse. His dark brown hair was sprinkled with gray throughout. "It's okay, buddy. It's okay. That was scary for me too." He stroked Connor's hair as he peeked behind them again.

Caleb hung his head while keeping pace with his dad. He had been really scared, too. Scared that he'd lose his little brother. However, the fear didn't take long to turn into resentment, hastened by his brother's tears and his dad's reaction to them. *Here we go again.* As soon as the thought entered his head, it began to hang even lower. Dad reached out and tousled his hair.

He picked his head back up a little and gave his dad a hint of a smile.

"Maybe I'll give you guys the bear spray to hold on to," Dad said.

The meadow where the attack had almost occurred was about a five-minute hike from their house, on a trail that the boys had mostly worn down themselves. The house came into view as they came out of the dense forest onto the stone path through their back yard. It was an average-size brown one-level house with a small back patio. To their right was a small chicken coop in the back corner of the yard. The chickens clucked and flapped their wings as the people entered the yard. Closer to the house on that side was Mom's garden, bursting over the edges of the raised beds. To the left was a huge weeping willow with branches raining down nearly to the grass. A raised, circular fire pit sat halfway between the willow and the house. Lawn chairs and s'mores sticks surrounded its grey brick walls.

As soon as they entered the yard, both kids bolted for the house to tell Mom what had happened. Caleb, being the older and the faster of the two, got there first. He slid open the screen door, "A wolf tried to kill us!"

"But Dad saved me!" Connor came in just behind his brother.

"What?" Mom said, a look of horror on her face as she turned around from the kitchen counter. She stood a few inches over five feet and had a medium build. Her shoulder-length, curly hair was light brown.

"It's okay, Amber, it's gone now, and not likely to come back," Dad stepped in and closed the screen behind him.

"It had a hurt leg."

"And it was really skinny."

"It got this close to biting me," Connor put his hands about a foot apart.

"Are you okay?" Mom knelt down on one knee beside Connor.

"Yeah, I'm still freaked out though." Connor started to chew his nails.

"I'm fine, too," Caleb said.

Mom looked as if she'd just remembered something important. She jumped up, grabbed the remote from the center island in the kitchen, and turned the TV off. The news had been on. "Well, as long as everyone is all right," she said, returning her focus to her frightened sons. "If you hadn't, uh, I mean, what'd you do, Spencer?"

"I yelled and threw rocks. Nailed it right in the face too. That's not easy at a full run. I still got something left

THE CREEK

in me." He gave her a reassuring look, ducking his chin
with his eyebrows raised. "I do hope it's okay though."

"Can we still let them…is it safe out there?"

"I think so. I told them to be more watchful out
there, right, guys?" He looked at the boys and waited
for nods of assent. "And I'm going to give the bear
spray to Caleb."

"Why him? The wolf came for me," Connor said.

"He's older, and he'll take care of you, right, Caleb?"

Caleb puffed up with pride and enthusiastically
nodded.

"Okay, it's time for dinner," Mom said. "You guys
get washed up and set the table."

They did as they were told and sat down to one of
their favorite meals: pan-fried chicken, mashed pota-
toes with country gravy, and corn on the cob from the
garden. The taste of the food that they already loved
was enhanced by their heightened awareness following
all the excitement.

"My snail finally won," Connor said between bites.

"Speedy Gonzalez, the fastest snail in all of
Mexico?" Mom said with a smile that seemed somewhat
forced; it didn't reach all the way to her brown eyes.

"Yeah, yeah, Shell Silverstein will get you next
time," Caleb muttered with his mouth full.

CHAPTER 2

The family sat wordlessly a while as they devoured dinner.

"I love you guys," Mom said with a sigh, shaking her head from side to side.

"Love you too, Mom," the kids replied.

"Can we have a fire pit and chill out for a little bit after dinner?" Connor asked.

"That sounds perfect," Mom said. Tears began to well up in her eyes. She stood up from the table. "I'll be right back, just a minute." She hastened to her room and shut the door. They could all tell she was crying behind it.

"What's up with her?" Caleb said.

"Well, she's probably just worked up a little about what happened," Dad said. "Hold on, let me go talk to her." He got up and followed her to their room.

Caleb couldn't quite place why, but he had a vague sense of dread. He rubbed his lucky rock in his pocket. It was a blueish flat rock about the size of a fifty-cent piece. A natural hole, about the diameter of a pencil, had been worn through it in the middle. It had once been his brother's lucky rock, given to him by his favorite nurse at the burn unit. She said it was supposed to help with the reoccurring nightmares that Connor had been having after the accident. It actually seemed to work, but Caleb figured it was due to the placebo effect, something he'd learned about in school. The nurse had called it a holy stone. Now it belonged to Caleb.

He glanced at Connor, who was biting his nails again, feeling the dread too. He put his hand on Connor's shoulder, feeling through his shirt part of the burn scar he'd had for nearly three years now.

Their cat, Punky, jumped up on Connor's lap. He rubbed her back near her tail. She raised her butt higher and higher until she tipped over. A hint of a smile appeared on his face. He looked up at Caleb, who was smiling back at him. Punky had been given to Connor as a kitten when he returned home from the hospital. The two were inseparable.

After a few minutes that seemed like much longer, their parents came back out of their room. They sat back down at the table to finish dinner. Caleb looked to them, anticipating an explanation.

"Sorry, guys," Mom finally said. "I'm just scared."

"It's okay, Mom," Caleb said. "We'll be fine."

She bit her upper lip, breathed out through her nose, then forced a smile.

They had been acting weird the last few days, but this seemed worse. Was she really this upset about the wolf? Caleb didn't think so. Something wasn't right.

CHAPTER 2

"Marshmallows?" Dad said.

"Yes, please." Connor stood up, gave his mom a long hug, and went outside.

They roasted marshmallows under a beautiful summer night sky. Caleb studied his parents' faces and actions as they sat around the fire pit. They both hardly said a word, and seemed lost in thought. Occasionally they would exchange glances. Dad gave her a little head-tilt toward the house.

"All right guys, let's call it a night," Dad said. He put the fire out and the four of them went back in the house. Both parents gave each of the kids a kiss on the top of their heads and they went to their room.

Caleb grabbed Connor and whispered, "Have you noticed that Mom and Dad have been acting really weird lately?"

"Yeah, I guess so," Connor said.

"They sleep with their window open in the summer. Let's go see if we can hear them talking."

They opened the back door as quietly as possible and crept outside.

Chapter 3

THE BOYS POSITIONED themselves right under their parents' open window. They could barely hear them talking inside. Caleb found himself holding his breath to try to hear better.

"It's getting worse," he thought he heard his mom say.

"How much worse?" Dad said.

Their cat rubbed up against Caleb's leg and started purring. He pushed her away, but she kept coming back. His parents were talking in hushed tones, and the purring drowned out much of the conversation.

"They can't know," she said.

"…don't want them to worry…" He only heard a fragment of what his dad had said.

Caleb strained to hear their words. It took every bit of his concentration.

"…spreading…" Mom said.

Punky meowed. He felt bad about it, but he flicked her ear. The purring stopped for a moment, then began again.

"…are very sick," Dad said? Or maybe, "You're very sick." Caleb thought it was the latter. His heart pumped hard and fast. His jaw clenched.

"Connor, could you take Punky away so I can hear?" he whispered.

"But I wanna hear too."

"Come on. I gotta know what's going on. I'll tell you everything."

"With what money?" his mom possibly said.

"Okay." Connor picked up the cat and carried her back toward the patio.

"…about as isolated as we can be…" Dad said.

"What can we do?" his mom asked.

"Stick with what we——"

Punky meowed again. Connor crept back and picked her up again. "Sorry, she got away."

"How can…" Mom started to ask. Caleb couldn't make out the rest of the question. This was frustrating. Blood pounded in his ears. He took a deep breath in through his nose and tried to concentrate again.

"…disconnect the TV. And we can——" Dad stopped, walked over to the window, and looked out. Caleb pressed himself against the side of the house and held his breath. Dad shut the window. Now Caleb couldn't hear a thing.

He crawled out from under the window, slipped back into the house, and snuck over to their door. He thought he heard both parents sobbing.

"I just want them to be happy," Mom said.

"Me, too," Dad said.

"I'll be praying," he barely heard Mom say.

He stayed by the door for a few more minutes but the conversation seemed to be over. Connor had knelt down beside him. He was frowning and his eyebrows were pressed together. Caleb motioned toward the door. Connor followed him down the path and a few feet into the forest.

"What'd they say?" Connor asked.

"I think Mom is sick," Caleb said.

"How do you know?" Connor looked worried. "How sick?"

"I'm not sure," Caleb said. "But I think it could be cancer. They said something about it spreading."

"No." Connor staggered backwards.

Caleb grabbed his shoulder. He was near panic too, but having his little brother to think about made him feel more in control.

"Mom said something about money," Caleb said, an idea of what was going on forming in his head. "Like they don't have enough money for the doctors or something."

"Probably because Dad lost his job," Connor said. Dad had been laid off from the Bellingham Fire Department a few months ago due to budget cuts. He told the boys he'd had several offers to work at other departments, but he took a calculated risk and turned them down because he didn't want to move. He said he loved living in relative seclusion in the woods. He told the boys he thought he could get a job closer to home, but it wasn't panning out yet.

Caleb sat down in the dirt. "They said something about shutting off the TV and some other stuff. To save money, maybe."

"What can we do?"

"I don't know."

"Should we tell them what we heard?" Connor said.

"Well, they really seemed like they didn't want us to know," Caleb said. "Maybe we should pretend we never heard anything. Maybe we can figure out how to help." A mental picture of him heroically bursting into the house with a case full of money flashed through his head. Mom looked so relieved and Dad looked so proud.

"Okay, I'll try," Connor said. "But I don't think I'll be very good at keeping a secret."

"Just keep it for a little bit," Caleb said. "Like I said, maybe we can figure something out."

The boys went back in the house and went to bed, but Caleb couldn't sleep. His mind was abuzz with worry. He tried to think of a way that he could get the money his mom needed. He couldn't come up with anything.

I could pray. It wasn't something he'd done since he was little and Mom used to make him and Connor say their prayers at bedtime. Now I lay me down to sleep, I pray the Lord my soul to keep, and if I die before I wake, I pray the Lord my soul to take. Those prayers had terrified him. He'd thought, *I could die before I wake*? The notion had never occurred to him until he'd been told to recite this. His feelings toward prayer had not improved since then.

They were no longer required to pray at night. But Mom had said that she'd be praying. Caleb thought it was worth a try. He wasn't sure how to start.

"I know I haven't done this in a while, but Mom could really use some help," Caleb whispered. "She's such a good person. She doesn't deserve this. And me and Connor need her to be alive. Could you please either take away her cancer or give us the money to cure her? Thanks, um, amen."

He doubted anything would come of it. He wasn't sure he even believed in God. He did when he was little, and Mom was really into church. But he had some serious doubts now. Mom stopped going to church soon after Connor's burn. He wasn't sure why she quit.

Caleb lay in bed thinking for what seemed to be hours. Sleep gradually overtook him.

*C*ALEB AWOKE WITH A START. He looked around his room, half-asleep. *Thank God. It was just a dream.* He had been ostracized by all of his classmates at school. Nate Pearson, the football team captain and most popular kid in his grade, had hated him for some reason. The details were starting to fade, but he remembered the sinking feeling when everyone took Nate's side and walked away from him. *She* was with the crowd too, and that maybe hurt the most. It had seemed so real. It wasn't as terrifying as the reoccurring dream about the ocean that he used to have when he was younger, but it was close.

His breathing began to slow to a regular rhythm. Outside it looked as if the sun had just risen. He lay back down and tried to go back to sleep. It was pointless;

his thoughts raced. He kept seeing her, turning away. The new girl, Ara, had moved here and started at his school a month before summer break.

I haven't even talked to her. Why do I care so——?

Mom! The thought jumped into Caleb's head and his feeling of relief disappeared. He was ashamed to be thinking, or even dreaming, of anything other than his mom's cancer. *What's the matter with me?*

"Caleb, are you up?" Connor stepped into his room wearing his Nightmare Before Christmas pajamas.

Caleb paused a moment, trying to decide if he was going to fake being asleep. "Yes, I'm up."

"I can't sleep," Connor said. "I keep worrying about Mom."

"Me, too," he said.

Connor shuffled over to Caleb's bed and sat down. "Wanna go get some eggs?"

"Sure."

Caleb slipped on some basketball shorts and the two went out to the coop and got a half-dozen eggs from the still-sleepy chickens. Caleb made scrambled eggs in silence while Connor made toast.

"I want to go back out to the creek to see if Dad killed that wolf," Caleb said. "And we can talk about Mom." His voice lowered to a whisper.

Connor shifted back in his chair, "Right now?"

"Yeah, why not?" Caleb said. "I'll leave a note for when they wake up."

Connor cleared his throat. "Okay." He went to his room and switched out his PJ pants for cargo shorts.

Caleb jotted down a quick note and they were off. As they approached the creek they scanned the area for signs of movement. Everything was still except for the busy early birds. Caleb searched the area where the rock had hit its mark. He picked up a jagged, baseball-sized rock. There was some dried blood on it.

"Check this out." He held up the rock to Connor, who had followed closely behind.

"Wow," said Connor. He eyed the meadow's edges.

They tried to imitate, from memory, the path that the wolf had taken to the forest. After several minutes they found some blood on some tall grass. Then a little more. Eventually they were able to track the path into the woods. They had followed the footprints and the occasional drop of blood for about a football field's length when they lost the trail in some dry underbrush. *The forest was awfully dry this summer,* Caleb thought. Dad told them that it was the hottest and driest summer he'd ever seen up here. Caleb couldn't remember the last time it rained.

They looked around the brush, but couldn't find any signs of the wolf.

"So he's still out there?" Connor asked.

"Yeah, I guess so," Caleb said. He looked in Connor's eyes. "But he won't be back here any time soon."

Connor's expression softened; his mind seemed eased for the moment.

"Did you have any ideas about what we can do for Mom?" Conner said.

"Nothing good enough. Did you?"

"We could sell our Playstation and our bikes and——"

"We couldn't even get a hundred bucks for that stuff," Caleb said. "Hospital bills cost thousands."

Connor looked down and his face reddened.

Caleb made his way back to the creek with Connor following close behind. They sat down creek-side, heads in their hands, thinking of something, anything, that could fix their situation.

Sitting and listening to the creek always calmed Caleb. Summers where he lived could be boring at times. Most of the kids in his school were bused in from a wide area. There weren't many kids his age around in the summer. During his brother's recovery from his burn injury, Caleb was alone a lot. In that time, he learned to appreciate a slower pace. He could sit out here and watch the babbling water go by for hours.

After his brother got better, they spent most of their lives in and around the creek. Back then, they loved wading up and down the water, pretending to be explorers. They would play hide and seek, climb trees, and catch and release all kinds of small forest creatures.

"A frog!" Connor said, jumping up and wading downstream. He bent down and caught a big greenish brown frog with both hands. "Look, it has four dark brown spots on its back in kind of a diamond shape." Connor was smiling.

"We don't have time for frogs right now," Caleb said, shaking his head.

"There's always time for frogs."

"Not when we need to be thinking of a way to help Mom." Caleb stood and walked toward his brother.

"Sorry." Connor crouched down and let the wiggling frog free on the bank.

"Let's go back and see if Mom and Dad are up yet." Just as Caleb was about to turn around and head toward the house, a gleam caught his eye. He saw something he'd never seen before on the bank of the creek.

"Hold on, Conn," he said as he made his way through the water.

He dug out the gleaming object from the mud. It was a small metal tube, roughly the size of a can of spray paint, with ornate caps at each end. The tube seemed to be made of tarnished copper that was mostly an aquamarine color. It seemed to have some kind of scene depicted on it, but time had all but worn it away. The caps were in slightly better shape and appeared to be made of silver to Caleb's untrained eye. They too had once been decorated, but like on the tube, any markings were just barely visible.

"What is it?" Connor said.

"Check it out! It's some kind of old metal container or something," Caleb replied, pulling at one of the caps. With much less effort than he had expected, the cap popped off. He put a finger inside and felt paper. He pressed his finger down and pulled out a stained sheet of parchment.

"Wow! What's it say?" Connor said.

"Hold on, hold on," Caleb said as he unrolled the paper, finding that it did, in fact, say something. It was written longhand in a style that he'd seen only in old movies. Some parts had been smudged and were unreadable.

They sat down on the bank, feet still in the water, and Caleb began to read aloud to his brother:

13th June, 1859

Clay Jr. And Samuel,

I take my pen in hand this night with much consternation in my heart. As I told your Mama in my last letter I had great success in the Fraser Canyon gold rush. But it has been plum difficult getting it home. I must admit the difficulty only began as ——————————————————————— ——————————————————— across the American border. I must have had one to many and let loose the detales of my fortune. I noticed that a fella overheard me and had me feelin powerful suspicious. So I snuck away that night and layed low in the woods. Sure——————————— ———————————showed up at my room intendin to rob me. Well I broke camp and headed for home right away. ——— them boys must have picked up my trail. I figure ——— about 8 hours ahead of them now, but they're closin the gap on me. They ain't gonna catch me, but just in case I'm gonna leave this letter at our Li'l Paradise right near the creek. I know you boys will be up here this summer with or without me. My hope is that if I don't make it back to you guys you'll come up here and — least have this treasure. God willing you'll find — note. I already stashed the gold somewhere so I could move faster. I'll leave you a few clues that only you two could figure out. I know how much you like pirates and treasure huntin' and stuff. I'll be damned if th——— guys are gonna get what belongs to our family! And boys, if I don't make it back, I want you to take care of your Momma and mind her. And tell her I love her very much. I love you boys so much it hurts. Will you do something for me? Will you promise to live every day, every hour, to the fullest? Will you live with joy and love in your hearts? Will you stick together as brothers, today and forever? Thank you. I hope that I'm on——— paranoid and I'll be home with you all soon! Then I can watch you try and figure out this treasure hunt I'm puttin together!

Clue #1
   Up, Way Up
   Our Family Will Be
   Etched for an Eternity

Affectionately Yo——

Your Loving Fath——

Clay Goodm——

"Do you think it's real?" Connor said.

"I don't know," Caleb said, thinking. "But…if this was really left here back then, and it was still here today…the treasure is still out there somewhere!"

"Yeah!" Connor rocked back and forth, beaming. "This could be exactly what we need for Mom!" He had renewed hope in his eyes.

Caleb felt it too. Energy coursed through his entire body.

But as Connor's words processed, he wondered how it could be that the possible answer to their problem had come so quickly. He thought about his prayer the night before. *Could it have actually worked?* Prayers had never worked for him before, not even little ones.

"But didn't he say the clues were something only they could figure out?" Connor asked.

"I know," Caleb said. "But we can *try* to figure them out. How hard can they be?" He examined the letter again. "Up, way up," he said to himself. He instinctively looked up and scanned the treetops as he rolled the parchment up and put it back inside the container. A huge bald eagle flew into his view from the north and alighted on the top of a tall cedar.

"So his kids never found this," Connor said. "That's kinda—"

"What are you girls doing?" A voice came from the path. Caleb recognized it immediately: Nate Pearson. Thankfully Nate couldn't see him yet. Caleb dropped the container and kicked it into the creek right as Nate emerged from the trees with a BB gun in his hands.

"Nothing," Caleb said. "What's up?"

"I'm bored as shit," Nate said. "Just out getting some of these loud-ass birds. What were you guys talking about?"

"Nothing," Caleb said again. "Just looking for snails to race." He impressed himself with the quickness of his cover-up. He shot Connor a glance that said, "Not a word!"

"That's pretty dumb." Nate was in Caleb's class, but stood a good two inches taller. He had shoulder-length blond hair and bright blue eyes that always seemed disgusted with the world they saw. "You playing football this year?"

"Yeah," Caleb said. "Probably. Are you?" He winced at his own stupid question.

"Of course I am," Nate said. "I'm the best guy on the team."

"Yeah, you are," Caleb said.

"We're going to a Seahawks game this summer," Connor chimed in.

"What, a preseason game?" Nate said. "That's lame."

"It's all we can afford right——"

"Shut up, stupid." Caleb glared at Connor then turned back to Nate. "Yeah, preseason sucks, huh?"

"This is great, but I gotta get back to killing," Nate said, heading up the creek toward his house. He lived about a mile away in an old, beat-up trailer with his mom. He was their closest neighbor.

"Later," Caleb said, trying to sound as laid back as possible.

Nate didn't respond.

Caleb turned back to Connor and noticed a hurt look on his face. "Sorry," he said. "But could you just not talk when he's around?"

"Okay."

Caleb was ashamed of how he acted around Nate. Caleb hated him, but at the same time wanted Nate to like him. Nate was popular at their small school because he was good at sports and he intimidated everyone. If you weren't friends with him, you'd have a tough time having any friends. The thought of that was too much for Caleb. And his brother always seemed on the verge of ruining things for him. When people his own age were around he just wanted Connor to go away.

The dinner bell rang out through the woods. Caleb retrieved the container out of the creek and put it in his pocket.

"Caleb, are we gonna tell Mom and Dad about what we found?" They started for home. "Maybe they could help."

"Not yet," Caleb said. "Don't you want to see if we can find it ourselves?" He had a vision of himself in a downpour, at night, with a shovel in his hand. Lightning crashed. He had found the buried treasure.

"Yeah, but if we can't find it we should tell Dad."

"Let's try to do it first," Caleb said. "For a day or two. We can go see what they want and then get back out here and start searching."

They arrived in the back yard to find Mom pulling weeds in the garden. "Hey guys, everything okay?"

"Yep, we just went out to hang out at the creek," Caleb said. "What's up?"

"In all the commotion last night we forgot to tell you that we were all invited to a birthday party."

"Whose?" Connor said.

"Ray Flores, our new neighbor's…"

Caleb's entire body tensed up; he didn't hear anything else she said. He was disoriented for a moment.

"She's in your class, isn't she, Caleb?" Mom's voice came back into focus.

"When?" He blinked hard. "Er, I mean who?"

"Araceli. Ray's older sister. I think she's in your class."

"Oh, yeah, Ara. I don't know her."

"Well, anyway, I thought it'd be nice if we went," Mom said. "They're new to the area. The parents didn't speak a whole lot of English but they seemed really nice. Your dad and I know a decent amount of Spanish anyway."

Options shot through Caleb's head. *How can I get out of it? Should I get out of it? Do I want to get out of it?*

"And you guys are going," Mom said, seemingly reading his mind.

"Will there be cake?" Connor said.

"Probably," Mom said. "We'll head over there in a few hours. They'll be serving lunch too. In the meantime I could use a little help with the garden."

Caleb went to his room and stashed the container under his mattress.

Chapter 5

"ARE YOU GONNA GO in your jammy shirt?" Mom asked Connor while they got ready to leave for the party.

"Yeah." He looked confused by the question as he let Punky out of the sliding glass door she'd been scratching on.

Caleb had changed into jeans and a blue plaid button-up shirt, the fanciest shirt he owned. With his shirt tucked in, it showed how long and skinny his legs were. He untucked it and smoothed it out.

"Did we get him a present?" Connor said, while making his way to the front door. He opened it, and within seconds, Punky came back inside. It was their routine.

"Yes, I went into town and got him a toy yesterday after they stopped by," Mom said. She probably meant Sumas on the Canadian border. That's what "town" usually meant. That or Maple Falls. Caleb preferred Maple Falls. Every time they went there they would stop at his favorite burger spot.

The family packed into their 1969 Chevelle station wagon. Mom had made a noodle salad and cookies and Dad brought a twelve-pack of Alaskan Amber. Dad pulled out of the driveway and headed down the quarter-mile of gravel road that led to the highway. Caleb always thought it was funny to call it a highway. To him it was only a winding, two-lane road through the forest with an occasional house or farm alongside.

As they pulled on to the paved road Mom said, "These trees are looking ready." Across the highway a Christmas tree farm extended as far as the eye could see. Neat rows of trees stretched from the road back to the hills in groups of varying heights. The group across from their driveway looked ready to cut this year. Caleb had always loved Christmas, but now he associated it with the accident. He stared out of the window at the lines of trees for the two-minute drive.

They pulled in the gravel driveway of a small, white house. There were three other cars in the driveway. Two big pots full of colorful flowers were on either side of the front door. Caleb gulped, took a deep breath, and got out.

Dad knocked on the front door.

A man in a white button-up shirt, jeans, and cowboy boots opened the door. "Hola, Spencer, welcome," he said and shook Dad's hand. "Please, come in."

Caleb nodded and smiled at the man as he followed his parents into the house. Wonderful smells of cooking food and strange music greeted them next. The atmosphere immediately appealed to him. Almost every square inch of the walls were covered with pictures of family or religious stuff. The accordion-laden music playing had a simple but catchy bass line and the singing, although foreign to him, had a feeling of happiness in it. A young woman holding a sleeping baby on the couch smiled up at him. He smiled back and then scanned around the house. The only other person he saw was a woman about Mom's age chopping vegetables in the kitchen. She put the knife down and stepped out into the living room to greet them.

"The people are out back," the man said after introductions were made. His name was Eutimio and his wife was named Maria. The woman on the couch was their oldest daughter, Isabella, with her baby Santi.

"Modelo?" he asked Dad.

"Sure, I'll try one of those." He held up his beer. "Tengo cerveza tambien."

"Órale my friend!" Eutimio said, slapping Dad on the shoulder. "Vaminos. There's carne asada ready out back."

The adults headed out into the back yard to eat and the boys followed close behind. Caleb braced himself.

As soon as he stepped onto the porch he saw her. She was every bit as tall and skinny as he was, but somehow it was graceful on her. Long black hair came down to the waist of her simple blue party dress. Her milk-chocolate eyes radiated warmth. She was making giant bubbles with some sort of wand. Three little kids were chasing after the bubbles, which were pushed around the yard by a gentle breeze. Caleb looked down at his shoes.

"No way!" she said. "Jack Skellington?" She stopped with the bubbles and looked at Connor.

Connor looked down at his shirt, then looked back up at her, eyes twinkling. "Yeah."

"I love that," she walked over to him.

He turned a little to hide the side of his face that was scarred. "It's my favorite movie."

"Mine, too!" she said. "Hi, I'm Araceli, but everyone calls me Ara."

"Connor," he waved at her. "That's my brother Caleb."

"Oh, hi." She looked at Caleb and gave him half a wave before she returned her attention to Connor. "I love all the songs. And how Jack tries to do good, but he just messes everything up. I feel like that sometimes," she said as the kids gathered around behind her and looked at Connor.

Caleb's heart dropped and his face reddened. He stared at Connor, the center of attention again.

"Hi, I'm Ray," one of the little boys said. He was almost a foot shorter than Connor. His head looked like it had been completely shaved a week ago. It was covered in a fine black fuzz. His eyes seemed just a little bigger than normal, like a drawing of a cute kid in a cartoon. "This is my party. I'm seven years old. What happened to you?" He pointed at Connor's face.

Now Connor turned red. "I got burned. A long time ago."

"Was it scary?" Ray said.

"Yes," Connor looked down.

The kids marveled at his scar. Caleb saw his brother struggling with the attention. Something told him he should intervene and direct the attention elsewhere. But he remained glued to his spot.

"I think it looks cool," Ray said.

Connor brightened a bit. The kids took Connor out to the yard and Ara began making bubbles for them again.

Caleb was left standing with his parents until Dad said, "Excuse us for a sec, buddy." Dad, Mom, and Ara's dad took their plates and went off to the side yard together. He felt awkward and exposed standing there alone. There were a few other adults standing on the porch and talking to each other, but he stuck out among them. His ears felt hot and he was sure they looked ridiculously red. He considered turning around and walking home but decided that would be even more embarrassing. He shuffled over to a large table that was covered with food. He put some charred meat and chips on his plate, then found a chair to sit in. He picked at his food. It was delicious but he just wasn't hungry.

He sat and rubbed his lucky rock until his thumb hurt. *A lot of luck this has given me.* He glared at Conner having fun in the yard. He was stuck in the familiar resentment that people were choosing his brother over him.

The only person to even acknowledge his existence in the first few days after Connor's burn was a
paramedic named Tavon Allen. On the ride in to the
hospital their mom had been frantic. She was holding
Connor's hand and whispering in his ear. There were
two medics in the back of the ambulance. One of them
was very busy at Connor's head. The other one was
busy too, but whenever he got a moment, he would
turn to Caleb and talk to him. Caleb was catatonic,
staring at a swinging IV bag that hung from the ceiling.
It was a long transport, and the second medic kept at
it. Eventually he got Caleb to talk. He told him that it
wasn't his fault, and that he shouldn't be so hard on
himself. He encouraged Caleb to keep his head up,
and said that he would come by and visit him at the
hospital some time.

Almost the entire first two days Conner was at
the hospital, Caleb was alone in the waiting room. He
understood that his parents were busy with Connor,
but he didn't really understand. He was eleven years
old. Paramedic Allen came in to check on Connor
the second day. He came into the waiting room first
and sat down by Caleb. He handed him a lollipop.
One of the flat, circular ones about as big as his face.
A semi-smile crossed Caleb's lips for the first time

since the accident. As he sat and talked with Caleb, the paramedic removed a pin from the lapel of his shirt and gave it to him. Caleb studied it, in awe, and thanked him for the gift. It was a red Maltese cross with a bar across the middle that said Paramedic. He loved that pin.

Within a year, he had lost it.

Connor had seen how distraught he was after losing his prized pin, so he gave his lucky rock to Caleb. "My nightmares have mostly gone away anyhow," he said. Caleb knew how nice this was, and how hard it must have been for Connor. At the time, he was very thankful for the gift.

In this moment, however, Caleb failed to see the pleasantness in his brother. He continued to focus on the fact that Ara had brushed him off to go hang out with Connor. His embarrassment turned to anger, and that anger, like many times before, was directed at his brother.

After about fifteen minutes, which seemed like much longer, he decided to go and see what his parents were doing. As soon as he turned the corner to the side yard all of the adults stopped talking, at once, and stared at him. They all had somber expressions.

CHAPTER 5

"Time for cake," Ray's mom yelled from the back door.

The kids stopped their game and rushed inside. The adults and Caleb followed. Once everyone was inside, Maria lit the candles on Ray's giant sheet cake. Caleb snuck a look at his brother, wondering if he'd wince or look away from the burning candles. He didn't. Ray's family began singing a birthday song in Spanish. Caleb snuck a look at Ara; he thought for a split second that she had been looking at him. She turned away so fast that he couldn't be sure. He immediately convinced himself that she hadn't been. When the song was over, Ray blew out the candles and everyone cheered. Caleb snuck a look at his parents. They were cheering and clapping with everyone but their eyes betrayed the joy they were trying to portray.

A woman who Caleb identified as Ara's grandmother seemed to be drinking much more heavily than the others. As the cake was being cut and distributed, she stood and started spouting off exitedly in Spanish. Several adults quickly grabbed her and ushered her away, admonishing her in whispers. Caleb had an eerie feeling flow through him. The only word he understood from her rant was, "Muerte." Caleb knew that meant death.

After the incident, and the cake, the party moved back into the yard for a piñata. The kids lined up from smallest to biggest and Dad goaded Caleb until he gave in and participated. When it was his turn, he broke the piñata with little effort. He was tall and skinny but had always been a natural athlete. The kids dove for the candy and coins that spilled out on the ground.

They stayed at the party for a few more hours, and during most of it Caleb wanted to disappear. He sat and listened to his parents talk to Ara's parents. From what he could pick up, between broken English, broken Spanish, and his distraction from always keeping a secretive eye on Ara, they had moved up here to Washington from Northern California. They had a relative up here and moved to pursue some kind of job opportunity. He didn't see Ara's grandma the rest of the time they were there.

Being around Ara was awkward. Especially when it seemed as if she was purposefully avoiding him.

He also needed to get out in the woods and start working on that first clue. When Mom finally told him it was time to go, a weight was lifted off of his chest.

They said their goodbyes and headed home. When they arrived it was almost five o'clock, and the boys made their way out to the creek as fast as possible to begin the search.

Chapter 6

"WHERE SHOULD WE look first?" Connor said.

"Somewhere high, obviously," Caleb said.

He went to the base of the giant oak tree that dominated the grassy meadow and started climbing. Connor followed. It was a climb they had done hundreds of times before and they effortlessly found themselves at the tree's highest climbable point. They searched the branches for manmade markings or anything unusual. Every branch sturdy enough to hold their weight was looked over, but nothing remarkable could be found. They climbed back down to the ground to reevaluate.

"Are you sure you didn't see anything?" Caleb said.

"Yes. I'm not stupid, I'd say if I saw something," Connor said.

"Sometimes I wonder," Caleb said. He started for the forest. "Come on, let's try going to the top of Skydiver Hill."

"Okay." Connor followed his big brother.

Skydiver Hill was about a mile north from their house. Caleb didn't know if it had an actual name, but it had been Skydiver Hill ever since their dad had helped rescue a skydiver who was caught up in a tree at the top of it. That was with his local volunteer fire district.

The trail there was barely visible. It had been cut mostly by the boys as well, but this one was far less traveled. Caleb liked to go up there from time to time, usually alone. There was a certain spot near the top where you could see out from the trees for miles. He would go out there and sit when he was feeling ignored.

"Why'd you say, 'Sometimes I wonder'?" Connor asked with half his normal volume.

Caleb kept hiking.

"Caleb, why'd——"

"Because you do stupid stuff sometimes."

"What did I do?"

Caleb didn't reply. He wasn't sure what his brother had done.

"What did I do?" Connor repeated, louder this time.

"Can't you ever find anything better to do than follow me everywhere?"

"I thought we were going to find this clue together?" Connor's shoulders drooped.

"I don't mean now," Caleb said. "Just, other times. Everywhere I go, you're there too."

"So you want me to go away?"

"Sometimes."

"Well, who would I be with?" Connor said. "None of my school friends live close to us. I don't like being alone."

"You got Mom and Dad," Caleb said. "They give all their attention to you anyway. Ever since…" Caleb stopped himself.

"Since what?" Connor said. "My burn?"

Caleb winced. "I don't mean that."

They had reached the base of the hill and started hiking up.

"I didn't ask to get burned," Connor said.

"Well, I didn't ask for it either."

"You hate me." Connor slowed down, his footsteps heavier.

"I don't hate you."

"Nobody really likes me." He stopped walking. "People at school think I'm a monster. They stare at me all the time. I hardly have any friends. And you want me to go away." He turned around and walked down the hill.

"Connor, wait," Caleb called. But Connor didn't stop.

He considered going after Connor, but knew it was pointless when he got like this. Caleb thought *Why am I like this*? As long as he could remember he'd resented his little brother. The fire had made things worse. Ever since then, it seemed like everything was about Connor. He hated the part of himself that resented Connor for the attention he got during his burn care. But it was a part of him he couldn't shake. Months in the hospital and months afterward his parents had all but forgotten him. *Of course they had to take care of him.* This battle had raged inside his skull for years now. But he was losing the battle. Especially after starting middle school. He needed friends, and to fit in. His needy, burned little brother held him back. *God damn it! It's not his fault.* But whether it was his fault or not, something in his mind told him it was the truth. He wondered *Do I even love him*? He wasn't sure. He used to, but now he thought that the feeling might be gone, possibly forever.

As Caleb hiked, his mind jumped back to school, friends, and fitting in with them. Trying to do that had done nothing but make his dad disappointed in him.

Last year at school he had been hanging out with Nate and another kid. The group had come around the corner and ran into William Larson. Nate started pushing him and calling him fat; the other kid joined in. Caleb stayed back, his dad's words echoing in his head. Nate said, "Come on, Caleb, you're letting this fat ass off the hook."

William gave him a look that said *Help.*

Caleb hesitated, then stepped up and pushed William. He pushed him harder than he meant to and sent him stumbling backwards until he fell on his butt. William began sobbing and curled on his side in a ball. Nate and the other kid roared with laughter and slapped Caleb on the back. He faked a smile.

Just then a teacher came around the corner and deduced what had happened. William refused to tell who had pushed him down, but Caleb admitted to it. He probably would have admitted to it whether he'd done it or not.

The absolute worst part was the look on his dad's face when he came to the school to pick Caleb up. He'd never seen so much disappointment. The long car ride home was in complete silence. When they arrived at home his dad just sat in the car. Caleb started to get out, but his dad said, "Stop." He looked at Caleb with the saddest look that must have ever crossed his face. "I've failed you."

Caleb looked down at his knees.

"I love you, buddy, but this is the most disappointed I've ever been with you." He cleared his throat. "What have I always told you about bullies?"

Caleb swallowed. "Never be one. And always stand up to one."

"Never be one." His dad let the words sit in the still air of the car for at least a minute. "How did that make you feel?"

"Like shit." The answer was instantaneous.

"Then learn something from this!" He smashed both fists on the steering wheel. Caleb gasped and his heart raced. His dad almost never yelled. Dad closed his eyes, took in a deep breath through his nose, and let it out slowly through his mouth. "Tomorrow I want you to find that boy and give him a heartfelt apology. And it had better be genuine."

The next day he sought out William and made the apology. He meant it, too. He'd never felt so ashamed of himself. William had accepted the apology. He sometimes helped Caleb in Algebra class since the incident.

That had been the worst he'd ever felt in his life, besides the day of the fire.

I'm pathetic.

His darting mind was interrupted by a different idea.

Mom.

He needed to forget about all this stuff for now and focus on finding that clue.

He was getting close to the top of the hill. He looked around for anything strange. He walked around the big tree at the top slowly, looking up. On the back side he could see what looked like carvings in the trunk. He felt a beat drop from the rhythm of his heart.

The carvings were too high for him to read, and they were obscured by a few small branches. He wasn't going to be able to climb up to see what it said. He searched the hill for something he could stand on, but found nothing. He knew he was going to have to go home and get Connor.

On the way back he cussed his brother for abandoning the search to go and pout. The excitement of

THE CREEK

finding the markings began to turn to anger. One negative thought fed on another and by the time he made it back home he had built up a rage. His fists were clenched, his face in a permanent frown, as he busted into Connor's room.

Connor tried to hide the piece of paper he'd been looking at behind his back. "What?" he said.

"What are you looking at?" Caleb said.

"Nothing."

"Let me see it." Caleb grabbed Connor's arm and tried to look behind him. Connor fought for a moment, but then gave in and handed the paper to Caleb.

Caleb snatched it away and looked at it. His shoulders crumpled, his arms fell down to his sides, and he stared at the floor.

Connor had been looking at the picture Caleb had drawn for him his first week in the Burn Unit. In crayon, Caleb and Connor stood hand in hand at the creek, the green meadow in the background, the sky blue with only two small white clouds, one of which partially covered the bright yellow sun. Connor had bandages over the right side of his face, neck, and body. Both of them had big smiles across their faces.

Caleb handed the picture back. He started to reach out and touch Connor's shoulder but stopped short.

He started to say something, but nothing came out. He stood in silence for a while. Connor remained quiet too, shooting quick glances up at Caleb.

"I found something up there," Caleb almost whispered.

"What?" Connor said, a hint of a spark in his eye.

"Some writing on a tree," Caleb said. "But I need your help to read it."

Connor sat up higher, with a small upturn in the corner of his mouth.

"It's almost dark," Caleb said. "But we can sneak out tonight after they go to bed."

"Okay."

Chapter 7

THAT EVENING SEEMED to take forever.

Their parents were still trying their best to hide something from the boys. But now that they knew the secret, it was so obvious that something was wrong.

Their dad was also trying to hide the fact that he was drunk, but he wasn't very good at hiding that either. He kept asking them if anything interesting was going on in their lives, and going on and on about how much he loved them. It was mostly his usual stuff, but there was a tinge of sadness behind his words. The alcohol seemed to keep the ideas flowing.

Their mom just wanted to be near them. She asked them to come sit with her on the couch. She held them both, wordlessly, and listened to her husband drone on. At one point she lay her head down on Caleb's shoulder. His chest welled up with emotion. He blinked away the tears that were trying to form and squeezed her tighter.

Caleb was reluctant to let this moment pass, but he was eager to get back to the hill. He waited for Connor to look at him and nodded toward their rooms.

"That was a long day," Caleb said. "I think I'm gonna hit the sack."

"Yeah, me too," Connor said with a big, fake yawn.

Their mom gave them each a longer-than-normal hug and a kiss on the head. "I love you," she said.

"Love you too, Mom," the boys said.

They looked to their dad. He had passed out, possibly mid-sentence, in the recliner. The boys and their mom shared a laugh, then the boys went to their rooms.

Caleb listened at his door. He heard his mom wake his dad. His dad said, "They're in bed?" There was a pause, then he said, "I think I messed it up." Caleb heard his mom make a shushing sound and corral him into their room. When he heard their door shut, he opened his own. He went to the hall closet and got two flashlights, the bear spray, a pen, and some sticky notes. Then he went to Connor's room.

"Ready?"

"Let's go."

They snuck out of the back door and made their way back up the hill. A few times on the way Connor thought he heard something out in the forest or behind them. They would stop and shine the flashlights toward the source of the noise, but couldn't see anything.

When they reached the top, Caleb caught a glimpse of movement behind the tree. He shined his light in that direction just in time to see a small animal scurry, or hop, away. "You're gonna stand on my shoulders and see what it says," he told Connor, putting the sticky notes and pen in his pocket. He positioned himself next to the tree with his hands on his knees.

"Sounds good," Connor said, climbing on to his brother's back. It was an awkward climb. He shimmied up the trunk with his hands while his feet struggled to find Caleb's shoulders. Caleb was surprised by his weight; he wasn't sure how long he was going to be able to hold him up like that.

"What's it say?" Caleb said.

"Hold on," Connor said, fishing the flashlight out of his other pocket. "It's really hard to read." Connor shifted his weight to the right, almost knocking his brother over.

"Steady," Caleb said. "Try not to wiggle so much."

"Sorry." Connor steadied himself, then carefully brought the flashlight up to eye level. "It's a heart with letters in it."

"Okay. What are the letters?"

"Inside the heart, on the top left side, it has C and G," Connor said. "On the top right it has AG. Bottom left is CG again. And there's an SG on the bottom right." There was a short pause, then Connor yelled, "It says *dig*!"

"*Dig*?" Caleb said, straining underneath his brother. "Inside the heart, too?"

"No, it's under the heart. And there's an arrow pointing down and a little to the right."

"Is that everything?"

"Uh…yeah, I don't see anything else."

"Climb down, then."

The climb down was even less graceful than the climb up. Connor fell and landed on his side. Caleb winced, expecting tears: he had landed on his burned side. Connor jumped up like nothing happened and pointed to a spot on the ground. "The arrow was pointing about here," he said.

Damn, Caleb thought. *We don't have a shovel, and it's a long way home and back.*

Connor dropped to his knees and started digging at the spot with his hands.

"You're not gonna get very far like that," Caleb said. But Connor was making much more progress than Caleb would have thought he could. He positioned his flashlight to shine on his brother's hands and dropped down to help. The dirt was really easy to dig up here.

They had dug down about a foot and a half when Caleb's hand struck something solid. "There's something here," he said.

The boys began furiously digging around the solid object. As they scraped the surrounding dirt from the hole the object started to take shape. Caleb pulled it out of the hole and brushed the dirt off. It seemed to be an exact replica of the tube they had found by the creek. He pulled off one of the end caps and reached inside. Out came another piece of parchment and Caleb unrolled it. This one was in better shape than the last one. Another, smaller paper fell out and floated to the ground. Caleb's eye barely caught it. He picked it up.

"Shine your light for me," Caleb said.

Connor pointed the light at the papers. The little one was cut into a triangle. It appeared to be one third of a map. There was a fancy arrow and an N drawn in the corner.

Caleb felt guilty for his thoughts, due to the seriousness of the situation with Mom, but this was exciting and fun. He tucked the map fragment behind the bigger note and began reading:

You did it!

I knew you would. But that one was easy. I figured you'd remember when we scratched our initials in that tree. This next one will be a little harder. You boys'll have to remember back to when your Momma taught you about the Roman times.

But first off, have you taken my words to heart about livin every moment fully? I sure hope so. This life is so precious. And love is the most important thing in the world. I know I sound like a blubbering fool sometimes, but I've found myself in this ridiculous situation and it has me thinkin a lot. I started thinkin, what am I doin? Wastin my time hidin these clues all over tarnation when I should be gettin away from them boys. But I stopped because I come to realize that I ain't afraid of death. The only thing I care about is my family. And I want to make this grand adventure for you boys whether it gets me closer to trouble or not. And like I said, this gold belongs to us! Besides, I'm too good out in these woods for them. This is like a second home to us and I'll have 'em spinnin circles tryin to find me out here. So with that in mind I'll get and leave you with these words. Don't be afraid to die. Be afraid to not truly live.

Oh yeah, tell your Momma I love her again and I can't wait to see her.

I know, I know, on to the clue!

Clue #2

WKH QHAW FOXH LV IRXQG ZKHUH OLWWOH PHHWWV ELJ.

WZHQWB SDFHV QRUWKZHVW. WKHQ VWRS DQG GLJ.

P.S. 3

Love Always,
Your Father

"PS3?" Connor said. "I thought this was from a long time ago, like, before PlayStations."

"No, it's P.S." Caleb handed the bigger paper to Connor. "See, like people write at the end of letters sometimes."

"Well. What is going on up here?" Nate appeared out of the trees with a flashlight in hand.

"Nothing," Caleb said instinctively as he dropped the map piece behind his back.

"You think I'll believe that you girls are up here in the middle of the night for nothing?" Nate said. "I saw your flashlights and followed you all the way up here." He looked at Connor, "What's that?"

"Nothing." Connor tried to shove the paper into his pocket but Nate snatched it from his hands.

Connor lunged to get it back but Nate easily held him off with one hand while he tried to read what it said.

Caleb froze. He absolutely needed to get that paper back from Nate, but he wasn't able to move. "What gold is he talking about?" Nate said. He pushed Connor backward, nearly knocking him down.

Caleb stood, silent and unmoving.

"Hey!" Nate said. "I said what gold is this talking about?"

"We don't know," Connor said.

"What is all of this?" Nate studied the letter. "What does this code mean?"

"We're not sure, we just found it," Connor said.

"Well, this seems like some kind of stupid game," Nate said. "But if there is real gold somewhere then it's mine."

He started to walk down the hill.

"Wait." Caleb's paralysis started to fade as Nate got farther away.

"What?"

"We know stuff that you don't know about the gold." Caleb was grasping for a reason to get his hands back on that parchment. "We found another clue. You'll need our help to find it."

Nate stopped. He looked back over the letter. "This does seem like gibberish," he said. "I guess I could let you figure this shit out, as long as you know that if we find it, it's mine."

"Okay."

"Caleb? We need that——" Connor started.

"Shut up, Connor," Caleb said. He hated to say that right now, but he needed Connor to keep quiet.

"Ha ha, come on, buddy," Nate said. "We're friends. Maybe I'll even give you a little bit of it, if there's enough. I know one thing: if you can find this I can about guarantee you'll be a starter next year."

"Cool," Caleb said. "Can I see that paper now?"

Nate handed it to him. "Now I know you aren't gonna be stupid and try to do this without me, right?"

"No way, man," Caleb said.

"Okay, well, give me a call when you figure this dumb-ass code out and I'll come meet up with you," Nate said, as he walked down the hill and out of sight.

"Sure."

Caleb was relieved to have the clue back in his hand. But now a whole new can of worms had been opened. How was he going to deal with Nate? They were going to have to be extra careful from now on. *And what if Nate finds out they were looking for it behind his back?* It would be social suicide next year at school, not to mention the beating he and Connor would likely get.

As difficult as it was going to be for him, he was going to have to push these thoughts out of his mind. Mom really needed that money. Because of Nate, time was a factor now more than ever.

"Sorry, Conn," Caleb said, picking up the map segment. "But I had a plan, and I didn't want Nate to know why we need the treasure."

"It's okay."

"We gotta get back," Caleb said. "We can figure this out tomorrow."

As he lay in bed, trying to fall asleep, his thoughts kept returning to how he had frozen up, again, on the hill. He was so ashamed of his inability to act in emergencies.

It wasn't the first time he'd been frozen like that. A little less than three years ago, two days before Christmas, he and Connor had been playing Candyland in the living room. His dad had been at work. He remembered everything about the house that night. The smell of the cookies his mom was making in the kitchen mixed with the scent of pine from the tree. Christmas lights flashed on the tree and overhead. "It's the Most Wonderful Time of the Year" was playing on the radio in the background. Candles were lit on the coffee table.

What happened next became a blur. He knew that Connor stood up and bumped into the coffee table. He saw his brother's face change first, from a happy expression to one of pure pain. Then he saw the flames crawling up from behind him. Caleb wanted to help, but he was frozen. He stood and watched as the fire grew. Connor was desperately trying to knock out the flames with his hands. Every impulse made Caleb want to do something, anything. But he couldn't move. Connor was screaming. Caleb knew the sound of that scream would haunt him.

His mom came running from the kitchen and picked Connor up in stride. She carried him to the front door and crashed it open with a dexterity no one knew she possessed. She threw Connor down outside in the snow and rolled him until the fire was out. She picked him back up and clutched him to her chest. He was still screaming in agony.

"Caleb!" she yelled.

"Caleb!"

He snapped out of his trance. "Yeah?"

"Call 911 right now," she had said.

That night had changed everything.

CALEB AWOKE TO THE SOUND of the house phone ringing. It was rare to hear that phone ring. He sat up and rubbed his face with both hands. He heard his mom answer the phone. A dream he'd been having was now fading fast. He thought he'd been trying to save a frog that was being tossed around in a stormy ocean. He ran out into the waves, desperate to rescue the frog, but filled with dread by the crashing of the water. The frog was always just out of his reach as he swam. Before he knew it, he had been pulled out to sea. In the dark. It had been terrifying.

The frog part was new. But being pulled out to sea was a reoccurring nightmare he used to have when he was a kid.

He heard his mom hang up.

He shook his head, as if trying to dislodge the nightmare, reached under his pillow, and retrieved the new clue. As he looked it over again, he heard a knock at Connor's door across the hall. That door had a familiar squeak when it opened. Caleb looked at the *P.S.* at the bottom of the letter. *Three, what could that mean?*

"No!" Connor cried from his room.

He heard his mom and Connor talking, His brother was sobbing. He got up and cracked his door. He could faintly hear them talking, but couldn't understand anything. After a few minutes, his mom left Connor's room and closed the door behind her. Caleb waited for her to walk away, then he stepped across the hall and knocked.

"Yeah?" Connor's voice was cracked.

"It's me," Caleb said.

"Okay."

Caleb entered and saw Connor crouched on the edge of his bed. Punky was on his lap, rubbing his chin with the top of her head. "What happened?"

"There's no camp this year," Connor sobbed.

"What?" Caleb said. "Why?"

"I don't know," Connor said. "Mom just told me somebody from Camp Tusbaye called and said it was cancelled."

Caleb knew how much this must hurt. That camp was so important to him.

When Connor was leaving the burn unit, he was told by one of the nurses about this summer camp for burn-survivor kids. The camp was sponsored by firefighters, "Like your dad," she had said. Connor really didn't want to go, but his parents thought that he should give it a try.

Caleb remembered going to drop Connor off at the camp. He felt bad for his brother, but was looking forward to a week-long break from him. Connor was quiet and shy, with his hoodie up to hide his face, and his eyes glued to the ground.

Then he remembered going to pick him up a week later. Connor had come running up to him in a t-shirt to give him and his parents hugs. Something had happened that week. Connor came out of the shell he had retreated into ever since the fire. Camp hadn't solved all of his brother's problems, but it did seem to give him a new outlook on life.

His second year at camp, Caleb got to come see him during the week on Visitor's Day. He was taken aback by the way some of the kids looked, and he tried his hardest not to stare. Some of the kids were burned really bad. A few were missing ears or fingers.

Caleb felt like crying at first, but after spending some time among the roughhousing and fun that they were having, he began to see things differently. These were just kids.

Connor took him on a tour through his cabin and down to the lake where they held their nightly campfire. He told Caleb about the songs they would sing, skits they would perform, and games they would play down there. Caleb couldn't help but feel jealous. He was surprised when Connor ripped his shirt off, like it was nothing, to go swimming. Caleb hadn't brought a swimsuit, so he sat and watched the kids splash and play. *Good for you*, he remembered thinking.

Apparently Connor's third year at burn camp was not going to happen.

"I never raised any money," Connor said, biting his nails.

"For the camp?"

"Yeah," Connor said. "Some of the older kids heard rumors last year that they maybe weren't going to have enough money, er, funding to keep camp running. They talked about doing fundraisers or something to save it. I was going to, then I forgot about it, and I never did anything." Connor shook his head, stroking the cat's gray fur.

"It probably wouldn't have made a difference anyway," Caleb said.

"I need that camp," Connor said.

Caleb sat next to his brother in silence.

Connor jumped to his feet, sending Punky scrambling awkwardly to the floor. "The gold!" he said. "Maybe if there's enough, we can save Mom and my camp."

"It's probably too late this year," Caleb said. Then immediately thought, *Why'd I say that?*

"Well...yeah, maybe, but at least I could help camp happen next year."

"Well, that's another reason to get it without Nate knowing," Caleb admitted with his head dropping down. Life as an enemy of Nate Pearson flashed through his mind. No football team, no friends, and no Ara. Not that he had a chance with her anyway. He saw a vision of himself with a bloody nose lying on the ground, Nate standing above him, his schoolmates gathered around, mocking him.

"So let's get to work on that clue then," Connor said.

They went back to Caleb's room and shut the door. He was reaching under his mattress when his eyes widened and he sucked in a quick breath. "The first tube," he said. "We need to recheck it to see if there's a map piece in there." He pulled it out from under the bed, opened it, and peered inside. Sure enough, there was a scrunched-up paper stuck down at the end. He pulled off the other cap and retrieved the paper. It was the second part of the map. He put the two pieces together, and realized that they were useless without the final part. The few, poorly drawn features on the map did indicate that the treasure was somewhere up north though.

"Let's focus on that code," Caleb said.

"There was a kid in my cabin last year, Tyler, that loved doing these codes," Connor said. "I'm trying to remember how he would make them." He stared at the code, then grabbed a notebook from Caleb's desk and rewrote it.

WKH QHAW FOXH LV IRxQG ZKHUH
OLWWOH PHHWV ELJ.

WZHQWB SDFHV QRUWKZHVW, WKHQ VWRS
DQG GLJ.

"Okay…so…first we figure out which letter shows up the most, I think." He started counting letters and scratching tally marks next to them.

Caleb stood and watched. It seemed like as good a place to start as any. He was glad, and a little surprised, that his brother had any code-breaking knowledge.

"So there are twelve Hs," Connor said. "That's by far the most. And the letter that is used the most in English is E. So we can try replacing the H's with E's." He crossed out the Hs and wrote in lower-case e's. "Uh…that's all I remember."

Caleb studied the new layout. An idea came to him. "The first word is three letters and ends in E, right?"

"Yeah."

"What if we try using 'the' for the first word?" Caleb said. "So W equals T, and K equals H."

"Yes, that's how you do it," Connor said, almost starting to smile. He made the corrections, substituting lower-case letters again, then rewrote the whole clue out.

the QeAt FOxe LV IRxQG ZKeUe OLttOe PeetV ELJ.

TZeQWB SDFeV QRUtKZeVt, theQ VtRS DQG GLJ.

"That's even more confusing," Caleb said.

"So what about this word?" Connor said, pointing to theQ. "The only letters that make sense for the Q are N and...Y."

"Or M," Caleb said.

"Oh, yeah."

"But something is telling me it's N," Caleb said. "Where it's at in the sentence, 'then' seems to make the most sense."

"Okay, we can try it." Connor made the changes.

the neAt fOxe LV IRxnG ZKeUe OLttOe PeetV ELJ.

TZenWB SDfeV nRUtKZeVt, then VtRS DnG GLJ.

"Well, that wasn't much help," Caleb said.

There was a knock at his bedroom door. Connor flipped over the notebook and Caleb tossed the letter under his bed. "Come in."

Their dad poked his head in. "What's up, guys?"

"Not much," Caleb said.

He looked at Connor. "Hey, buddy, I heard about burn camp, I'm real sorry to hear about that." He came in and gave Connor a hug. "Unfortunately guys, I've got more bad news."

Caleb held his breath.

"I was going to wait to tell you, but we may as well get it out now," Dad said. "You know the Seahawks game we were supposed to go to in a few weeks? Well, we can't do that anymore."

Caleb glanced at Connor with a knowing expression. Connor shot him back a look that told him they were on the same page. This was another money issue: it had to be. Caleb was bummed, but he had bigger things to deal with.

"It's okay, Dad," Caleb said.

"Yeah, it's okay," Connor stepped forward and gave his dad another little hug.

"I'm sorry, you guys," Dad said. "I was really looking forward to doing that with you."

"We were too." Caleb gave his dad half a smile.

"You know…you boys are the best," Dad said, a little choked up. "Some kids would have thrown a fit about this, but you two took it in stride. Thank you for being you."

"Who else could we be?" Connor said.

"Yeah, I just feel so lucky sometimes, even——." He stopped himself and paused. Trying hard not to show emotion on his face, he said, "I've got to go down to the station for a while. We have a red-flag warning, some bad weather coming through. So I'll see you guys later. Stay safe today, please."

Dad had been laid off from his full-time job as a firefighter, but he still volunteered with the local fire district.

"Okay," Caleb said. "You stay safe, too."

He gave a half-hearted smile and left the room, shutting the door behind him.

Connor flipped the notebook back over.

"So what could the three mean?" Caleb asked himself aloud. "And what could it have to do with Roman times?"

"I don't know much about Rome," Connor said.

"Me, neither," Caleb said. "Just like gladiators, the coliseum, and Caesar."

"Caesar?" Connor's face was scrunched up, thinking hard.

"Yeah, what about him?"

"I'm trying to remember, but Tyler called this code a Caesar something," Connor said. "And...I think he would take the alphabet, then move each letter over a few spots."

"Three!" Caleb said. "What if we're supposed to move three spots?"

They looked down at the notebook. Caleb counted three spots away from the first letter of the code, W. Moving forward made it Z, but moving three letters back made it a T.

"We got it," Caleb said, giddy with anticipation.

Connor wrote in the new letters carefully. Real words were forming on the page now. When he was done, he read, "The next clue is found where little meets big. Twenty paces northwest, then stop and dig."

Caleb's excitement faltered. He had hoped the unraveled code would tell them where it was. Instead they got another cryptic clue to figure out.

"Where does little meet big?" Connor said.

"I have no idea."

CALEB FIGURED THAT the only way they were going to find "where little meets big" would be to go and explore the woods. They were headed out of the back door to do just that when their mom stopped them.

"I made you breakfast," she said.

"Thanks, but we're not hungry," Caleb said.

"But I made you French toast and bacon."

The boys stopped, unable to resist. They came back and took a seat at the table.

"Ha, I knew I could get you to spend a little time with me," Mom said.

"We want to spend time with you," Connor said. "But we have a lot to do."

"Oh?" Mom said. "Like what?"

Caleb put a finger up to his pursed lips. Mom had her back turned to them.

"Hiking…and another snail race," Connor said. "Caleb wants a rematch."

"Oh, I see," Mom said. "Very important stuff for sure."

She came to the table, served them their breakfast, and sat down to eat with them.

"Are you doing okay, Connorific?" Mom said.

"Yeah," Connor said. "Still sad though."

"I understand."

"Why does God do stuff like that?" Connor asked. "That camp is nothing but good, and he is going to allow it to be shut down? And you…er, I just don't understand that."

"That's a tough one," Mom said. "I'm not sure I have the answer for you. I could say, 'God works in mysterious ways' or, 'He has a plan that is beyond our understanding.' But I know what a frustrating answer that can be."

"Do you still even believe in God?" Caleb had wanted to ask her for a while.

Mom paused. "Yes, I do."

"But we don't go to church anymore," Caleb said.

"No, we don't." She took a moment, then said, "We went to a very strict church. It was the church I was brought up in. I never knew any other way. When I met your father, I think I slowly began to see that maybe my church didn't have all the answers. He never tried to talk me out of Christianity; it wasn't that. But seeing my parents' reaction and the church's reaction to my falling in love with a non-Christian didn't sit well with me. The constant talk of hellfire and brimstone no longer appealed to me either. But I stayed in it. And after we had you guys, we continued to go, even though I had so many doubts in the back of my mind."

"So what made you quit?" Caleb said. Another thing he'd been dying to know.

"Well, after Connor's accident." She reached out and held Connor's hand. "Some things were suggested from some of the people, and even the leadership, that turned me off from ever returning there."

"Like what?" Connor said.

"I'd rather not repeat such ignorant bullshit," she said.

Caleb was shocked. Mom almost never cussed. "So did you stop believing then?"

"No," she said. "But for a little while I thought I might be losing my faith. Actually, for about two years."

"What changed?"

"I was completely disillusioned with my old church, and really with organized religion in general," Mom said. "But I never really stopped believing in the power of Jesus' love. It's something that rings true at my core. So I chose to focus on that instead. And, like I've told you before, I really hope that you can give that love a chance in your hearts."

"I try," Caleb said. "But I'm just not sure if I really believe it."

"All I ask is that you give it one more try," Mom said. "I don't want to pressure you too much, and I understand your reluctance, but it's important to me that you truly give it another chance. Both of you. Please?" She tried to say this casually, but the look in her eyes showed that this was an important immediate thing for her.

"I will," Caleb said.

"Me, too," Connor said.

"Thank you," Mom said. "I'm so glad you brought God up this morning, Connor. I've been meaning to talk with you both about this anyway, so this was perfect."

The boys were finishing up their breakfast.

"If you were going to do something great, and really help somebody, would you tell them about it first? Or do the great thing first?" Connor said.

Caleb gave his brother a questioning look.

Mom paused. She seemed to be struggling to find an answer to this question. "I guess I would do the great thing first."

Caleb was relieved that she answered that way. He was worried Connor was going to spill the beans if she'd gone the other way. He still thought that finding the treasure first, before telling them that they knew about the cancer, was what they should do. If he was being honest with himself, part of the reason for hiding that they knew the truth was that it made it less real. Part of him still didn't really believe that she was sick, —she didn't seem sick. But telling her that they knew would somehow cement the idea in his mind.

"All right boys," she said. "Thanks for having breakfast and chatting with me. Now go have fun. But stay close: your dad says there could be a storm coming in."

They gave her a quick hug and headed outside. Caleb grabbed his mom's little flowery-handled trowel from one of the garden boxes just in case. He tucked it into the waistband in the front of his shorts. They made their way out to the creek to look around and think.

The short walk out to the meadow had already made Caleb thirsty. As he knelt to get a drink from the stream he noticed that the rocks on the bank that were not hiding under the cover of the mossy trees were hot to the touch. Sweat beaded up on his forehead.

Caleb wiped his brow and scanned the meadow. He thought that the giant oak tree could be the "big" thing, but was unable to find anything little meeting it in any way. What else was big nearby? He considered Skydiver Hill for a moment, but that couldn't be it; they'd just found the last clue there. There was the "lake" further north, that was pretty big. *There could be something to that*, he thought as he wandered around the meadow.

"Hola," a small voice called from the path.

Caleb turned toward the voice. It was Ray, wearing cutoff jean shorts and nothing else, not even shoes. His sister Ara, wearing black shorts and a dark grey tank top, followed about ten feet behind him. Caleb felt adrenaline shoot through his body, but it was diminished this time. He had so much important stuff on his mind that it was almost as if he didn't have the time to be his usual scared-to-death self around her right now.

"Ray!" Connor called. The two had formed an instant friendship at the birthday party. "Ara!" He'd obviously formed a bond with her too.

"Hey Connor, hey Caleb," Ara said.

It was the first time he'd ever heard her say his name.

"Hey Ara-celi," Caleb stuttered.

"Just Ara is fine," she said with a smile.

"What are you guys doing?" Ray said as he jumped, belly first, into the creek. It was a perfect day to swim, although storm clouds could be seen gathering to the west.

"Can I tell them, Caleb?" Connor said. "Maybe they could help us. They're really nice."

Every possible outcome of letting them in on the secret seemed to blast through his brain. Even though most would probably lead to disaster, he found that he was eager to tell someone else about it. Keeping secrets wasn't easy, and besides, this could be an excuse to hang out with her.

"Sure," he told his brother.

"We're looking for a treasure," Connor said. "A real one."

"What?" Ray jumped up from the creek and ran over to them.

"Seriously," Caleb said. "We found this old metal tube in the creek bank, right here. There was an old letter from the 1800s inside, that this guy wrote to his kids. He had a ton of gold and hid it for them. Then he left some clues for them to find it."

"Why did he hide it?" Ara said.

"I guess there were, like, bandits chasing him, trying to steal it," Caleb said. "So he said he was going to hide it just in case. But it also seems like he was having fun and wanted his kids to have an exciting treasure hunt."

"That's the awesomest thing I ever heard," Ray said.

"So what's the clue say?" Ara said.

Caleb fished the notebook paper from his pocket and handed it to her. "We had to decode the message, but now we're stuck."

"Le'me see." Ray crowded Ara and she read the clue to him.

"I was thinking it might be the lake," Caleb said.

"Well, let's go." Ara handed the paper back. "Where is the lake?"

"It's not actually a lake. More like a big pond, but we always called it a lake when we were younger. It's a few miles north of here."

"Vaminos," Ray said. "I mean, come on, let's go."

"You don't have shoes," Connor pointed out.

"He never wears shoes," Ara said. "He's got some tough feet."

"Why?" Connor asked.

"I don't know," Ray said. "I just don't like 'em."

Caleb had some doubts about hiking all day in this crippling heat with a kid with no shoes and his sister, without water, food, or even the bear spray. But those doubts proved to be no match for the sense of adventure that permeated him. It would have been an easy trip back to the house to get some supplies, but the moment was now. The man in the letter kept telling his kids to live every moment to the fullest; that advice was finding a foothold.

"This way," he said.

He started north on the sparse trail that led to Skydiver Hill. Once there, he knew of a better trail that went northeast from the hill to the lake. He looked to the sky in the west. Storm clouds were building, but he hoped they weren't headed their way. His dad had taught him always to be prepared, to watch the weather, and always to be aware of your surroundings while hiking. If this were a normal day, he'd have had to call off the hike. But this was far from a normal day. He refused to sit and do nothing when there was a treasure to find, and their mom to save.

"If we find the gold, I'm going to buy a new hat for Papa, a bracelet for Mama, and a bike for me," Ray said.

"What about me?" Ara asked, giggling.

"Oh yeah, well, what do you want?"

"Oh, nothing really," Ara said. "It's not gonna be our gold anyway. We're just along for the ride."

"We'll split it with you," Caleb said, without thinking. "If there's enough, I mean."

"Enough?" Ray said. "Enough for what?"

Caleb and Connor looked to each other, Connor's look seemed to say *We've come this far, might as well tell them everything.*

"Well, our parents had been acting really weird for a few——"

"Our parents have been acting really weird too," Ray said.

"For at least a week now," Ara said. "But, sorry, go on."

"Hmm." Caleb paused. "So, anyway, we snuck out under their open window and heard them talking. And…we think our Mom has cancer."

"Oh no." Ara reached over and touched Caleb's shoulder.

"Our dad got laid off from work," Connor said. "So they can't afford the hospital bills and stuff. That's why we need to find this treasure, fast."

"I don't need a new bike, I have an old one that Papa can fix," Ray said.

Ara gave her little brother a look that sang love.

Then she turned to Caleb and Connor and said, "We're in, all the way. However we can help."

"Thanks." Caleb's face lit up in the most genuine smile he'd had in a week.

"I told you they were nice." Connor punched Caleb on the shoulder.

Thunder rumbled nearby. They all looked up, but couldn't see the thunder's source through the forest canopy. Caleb picked up the pace and the others followed. Before long they reached the hill. They had to traverse a dense thicket of dry underbrush in order to find the other trail. Caleb thought that Ray was going to have trouble making it through. He was pleasantly surprised to see him scurry through the brush like Br'er Rabbit. After a short search, the trailhead was found, and the journey resumed.

Chapter 10

THE THUNDERSTORM WAS NOW nearly overhead. Caleb quickly considered their options as they continued toward the lake. They could turn around now, but the thunder cell would probably pass over them before they made it home. That wasn't a real option for him anyway. If they continued down the trail, they risked getting struck by lightning out in the open. He knew that the cells usually traveled fast. Maybe they could let it pass them by? If they hunkered down in the forest they shouldn't have to worry about getting struck; they'd probably get drenched, but it was a hot day and getting wet didn't seem so bad.

CHAPTER 10

"Let's stop here and try to find some shelter," Caleb said. "We can let this storm pass over the top of us, then keep going up to the lake."

Ray's happy-go-lucky demeanor faded away and was replaced by a skittish uncertainty. He jumped every time he heard thunder and clung to his older sister. Connor and Ara still looked competent and capable.

Advice from Caleb's father was coming back to him. Proud that he was able to recall what he'd been taught in this hectic moment, he searched for a small stand of trees or a low area to hide in. The terrain sloped downhill just to the right of the trail. It continued down about thirty feet to where it formed a small ravine with a downslope from the other side. Littered throughout the bottom of the ravine were several small birch trees. It was perfect.

Caleb started down into the ravine. "This way, guys."

The others followed close behind. When they arrived at the bottom they saw a bright flash of lightning close by. Caleb counted aloud, "One, two, three, four, five." Thunder shook the air around them. "I think that means the last strike was about a mile away."

"I can't remember what Dad told us to do," Connor said.

"We need to duck down, like this." Caleb crouched down with his heels together. "Then tuck your head between your legs and cover your ears with your hands." He followed his own instructions and the others mimicked him.

"That's it?" Ara said.

"Yeah," Caleb said. "It should pass over us pretty soon."

It was then that Caleb noticed something that he found strange. It wasn't raining. He'd never experienced a thunderstorm without rain. He didn't have much time to ponder this. A lightning bolt struck the ground on the other side of the trail with a fantastic crash, about a football field's length away from them. The sound was deafening, like a gunshot going off near his head. The ground exploded, sending earth and brush flying through the air. Some of that brush was on fire. As it fell back to the ground it lit the dense, dry underbrush all around it. Caleb felt a cool powerful wind rush over him. At the same time he saw that same wind spreading the fire in all directions.

"Run!" he yelled, grabbing his brother by the arm. But Connor didn't budge. "Connor, come on, we have to go! Now!" He pulled his brother's arm, but Connor remained transfixed by the fire, staring at it with a look of sheer panic on his face.

"Run, Connor, run," Ara yelled at him. She looked to Caleb, silently pleading with him to do something.

"Come on, Connor." Even Ray ran over to him and tried tugging him away.

Caleb decided he was going to have to carry him out. He didn't know if he would be able to handle the weight, or if he could even come close to outrunning a fire while carrying his brother.

As he bent forward to scoop him up, he noticed a dramatic change in Connor's appearance. Instantly his face went from that of a frightened little boy to a look of sheer determination. It was as if he had fought a battle in his mind in that moment and won.

"Let's go," Connor said, grabbing little Ray by the arm. Caleb could tell that this was going to be a defining moment for his brother, if they could make it out of this alive.

All four of them ran away from the greedy, building flames. They ran up the other side of the ravine and kept going, roughly eastward. Caleb glanced back. A roaring wall of orange engulfed the entire forest behind them.

He thought his heart was going to beat out of his chest as they fought through the brush that covered the landscape in front of them. They struggled over and under fallen trees as the fire gained on them. The brush and other obstacles that hindered their escape were fueling the fire even more. The wind was relentless, blowing fiery embers past their heads, and pushing the flames at an unbelievable rate.

Caleb tripped over a rock that was concealed in some tall grass. Connor stopped to help, but Caleb jumped right back up and kept running. Ara had a hold of her brother's hand with an unbreakable grip. She pulled him along at her speed, lifting him over anything in the way.

It was starting to feel hopeless. Caleb's lungs screamed for air; he wasn't sure how much longer he could run like this. The fire showed no signs of slowing down. In fact, it seemed to be picking up speed.

This is what it's like to die, Caleb thought. Panic raced through him. The heat was becoming unbearable on his back. "Please, help us," he said to himself.

He heard something up ahead. A rushing sound, not unlike the raging fire behind him. *Are we surrounded?* The thought appeared just as they shot out from the forest into a small clearing. The sound he had heard was the river. *We're saved*, he thought. The river was white with freezing, churning water. *Or are we?* It surged over and around giant boulders with raw power. Still, the river's fury was inviting compared to the idea of burning alive. A quick look at everyone else confirmed that they were all on the same page.

He looked at Ray. "Can you swim?"

"No," Ray said, looking back at the fire, then jumping in the river.

"Float on your butt, feet pointing downriver," Caleb barked as he jumped into the rapids after Ray. Another pointer his dad had given him.

The water pushed him downstream so abruptly that his neck whipped back. The freezing cold took his breath away. His right foot smashed into a rock. He tried to push off of it, but didn't get far. His right hip slammed into the same rock, sending pain shooting up his side. He strained to look behind him to see Connor and the others. He caught a glimpse of his brother and Ara. They seemed to be floating all right. He saw the flames jumping over the river and igniting the brush on the other side. He faced forward and was immediately pulled under water. His arms flailed as he tried to bring his head back above the surface. He was being tossed around in all directions;

he couldn't tell which way was up. The trowel in his waistband cut into his belly as the water folded him in half. He fought for a handhold, for a foothold, for anything that could bring him up to the air. His lungs burned. The top of his head hit something solid. He felt like he was starting to lose consciousness. He must have been under for minutes now. The world began to go dark.

His foot touched something that felt like it could be the riverbed. He moved to put both feet against the ground, and pushed up with all the strength he had left. His head shot out above the water. He gasped in a lung-full of air.

He was being carried on the surface now. He pointed his feet back downriver and gulped in fresh air as fast as he could.

Eventually the river became wider and slowed down. He was able to look around and get his bearings. To his right was a shallow pool of almost still water. He swam as fast as he could toward the pool. The river was carrying him past it, and he was afraid he wasn't going to make it. He was almost out of energy when he tumbled out of the current, and into the stagnant pool. He stood up and waded to the riverbank. He turned to the water, searching for the others.

"Caleb," a cry came from upriver. To his great relief, he saw Connor and Ara standing together on some rocks about a hundred feet away. "Have you seen Ray?" Ara called.

"No," he called back. His heart was in his throat. He scanned the water for any sign of Ara's brother. Nothing. He looked back to Connor and Ara. They were desperately surveying the river too. Caleb felt helpless. *What could they do?* He started walking along the bank, downriver, while keeping his eyes hyper-focused on the violent rapids. "Ray," he called. No answer. A vision of Ara, crying and inconsolable, appeared in his mind's eye. "Ray!"

He came around a giant rock on the bank and saw him, lying face-down in mud. Dread filled Caleb's chest. He ran to Ray, crouched down, and lifted him to sit against his knee. His eyes were closed; Caleb couldn't tell if he was breathing. Caleb closed his eyes and racked his brain for what he should do. He'd been taught CPR, but was struggling with what he should do first.

He put his ear to Ray's mouth and watched his chest for the rise and fall. Nothing.

Just as he was about to pick his head up and make an attempt at pushing on Ray's chest, a gush of water splattered against his ear, followed by several deep coughs. Ray's little body convulsively curled forward as the coughing continued. He went down to his hands and knees in the mud. After a few moments, he looked up and flashed a faint smile. Relief flooded over Caleb. He jumped up and motioned for Ara and Connor. They came running down the bank. Ara picked up her little brother and held him tight. Caleb and Connor almost embraced each other, but both of them stopped short of actually touching.

"Your head is bleeding," Connor said.

"Your face is bleeding," Caleb replied. Connor had a cut across his cheek, opposite the burned side.

They checked themselves over, finding many cuts and scrapes on their arms, legs, and bodies. Now that he had a moment to think about it, Caleb's hip throbbed.

He turned northward, checking on the fire. They must have floated a long way. The smoke was thick, but seemed very far away. The wind was out of the south, so they should be safe for now, Caleb thought. He felt a hand on his shoulder. It turned him back around, and into an awkward hug.

"Thank you," Ara said in his ear.

"I didn't do anything," Caleb said. "I just found him."

"Well, thank you for finding him, then." She stepped back, flashed him a smile, then looked down at the rocks.

Caleb looked down too. He felt that his face must have been bright red. His hand thrust into his pocket and he clutched his lucky rock.

"I'm not sure if that was the scariest, or awesomest thing ever," Ray said.

"Maybe a little of both." Caleb was glad someone had said something.

"Definitely both." Connor exuded a subtle confidence that Caleb had never seen in him before.

Chapter 11

"WHERE ARE WE?" Ara said.

Caleb looked around. This part of the river was very familiar. A little ways down the river, he saw a creek emptying into it. Overhead, the last storm cloud passed by the sun. The river valley was filled with bright, warm light.

"That's Empyrean Creek!" Caleb said.

Ara and Ray gave him inquisitive looks.

"Our creek, the one that goes by our houses. We've been here a thousand times," Connor chimed in.

"So we can just walk down to where the creek meets the river, then follow it back home," Ara said.

"I like that idea, get away from this big scary river, and follow that nice little creek." Ray started walking downriver. He stopped and spun around. "Wait a minute. Little creek, big river. Where little meets big? Could that be it?"

"Yes." Connor ran to the smaller boy, picked him up, and whirled him in circles.

"That's gotta be it," Caleb said. "Nice work, Ray."

The four of them hurried to where the creek met the river.

"Twenty paces northwest, then stop and dig," Connor said from memory.

Caleb limped out twenty paces, as close to northwest as he could. Wild grasses grew on the spot, so he pulled them up, clearing a small area. Then he pulled the trowel from his waistband and started digging. The dirt was packed hard here, and it was very rocky. He was glad that he'd grabbed the trowel from Mom's garden, even if it had cut him.

It was slow going. After several minutes he had dug down about one and a half feet, finding nothing but rocks. He passed the trowel to Connor, who dug another foot and a half. Ara took a turn, followed by Ray. By the time they were finished they had dug out a four foot by four foot area a little more than four feet down. They still hadn't found anything.

"Maybe we're in the wrong spot," Connor said.

"It was buried over a hundred years ago," Caleb said. "Maybe the creek altered its course during that time. Or maybe it's further underground."

"Or maybe your paces weren't big enough," Ara said as she walked back to the mouth of the creek. She turned and stretched out her long, skinny legs to pace it off again. When she reached nineteen she stopped. She was already a few paces passed the hole they had dug. "There's a frog in the way," she giggled. The frog hopped away and disappeared into a marshy area before Connor or Ray could get a good look at it. Ara took one final giant step and said, "Let's try here."

The spot that she had come to was bare dirt, with a few pine needles on top. Mom's trowel met far less resistance here. In little more than a minute Caleb had dug about two feet down and struck something that wasn't a rock. In fact, it sounded like metal. He dug around it and pulled up another identical metal tube.

"Got it!" he said. The others crowded around as he popped the cap and pulled out the paper inside. There were two papers again. The last piece of the map, Caleb thought. There on the third map piece was a big, red X drawn just north of the lake. His chest tingled with adrenaline. He unrolled the other page and read the note aloud to the group.

You guys are good!

You remembered the Caesar Cipher. I knew you'd get it.

You now have all 3 map pieces! I trust you'll be able to find the X marks the spot. I felt like a pirate drawin up that map, pretty fun! Speakin on fun, are you boys squeezin the fun out of life? Are you squeezin the joy out of life? I can't stress that enough. Even when the world throws trouble at you. The way I see it, you can live one of two ways. You can see the world as cruel and unfair, see the worst in your fellow man, and become bitter. Or you can see the world as beautiful, see the best in people, and be happy. Terrible things happen, but wonderful things happen too. What you choose to focus on is up to you. Life will throw you problems, its how you deal with them that makes you who you are.

Sorry about the ramblin again. I should have been tellin you boys this kind of thing all along instead

of writin it down now. But I ain't much of a talker, and
I'm findin it easier to write rather than say.

So the clue this time is for when you get to the X.

Last Clue
You've found 3 of my tubes, but you'll need to find
one more.

The last is hidden up in a tree, just north of the
shore.

Drop a rock down through that tube, and mark
that very spot.

A bee line from the nearest birch, and a line
you've got.

50 feet out usin that line, goin the other way.

All our gold is hidden there, what a glorious day!

Haha! You didn't know your Pop was a poet!
Love to your Momma, of course!
I Love You Two.
Your Father

Caleb again felt a surge of excitement, followed
by guilt. This was the most fun he'd had in his life. At
times he found himself forgetting the grave nature of
the situation. When it came crashing back he couldn't

help feeling ashamed. But why couldn't this be fun and productive? Being somber wasn't going to get them to the gold any faster. The man's words were connecting with him. Life had put an obstacle in their way, a big obstacle. But they were taking equally big steps to overcome it. And if they had fun along the way? Even better, he was beginning to believe.

"We have to go back to the lake," Ray said.

"Not today, hermano," Ara said. "It's getting late."

"Yeah, we'd better go home," Caleb agreed. "We can go to the lake first thing tomorrow, if the fire is over, that is."

"Ugh! I can't wait," Connor said. "Isn't this exciting?"

"Sure," Caleb said plainly. He always felt the need to counterbalance whatever emotion his brother was feeling. If Connor was excited, his excitement tended to dull. He wasn't sure why it happened, but it almost always did. He was glad to notice that it was less pronounced than usual this time.

"I can't wait either," Ray said.

"This *is* pretty exciting," Ara said, wringing her hands together and flashing a toothy grin.

The sky darkened. They looked up to see that giant, black clouds had rolled in from behind the last storm, obscuring the sun's brief appearance. Thankfully, there didn't seem to be any thunder or lightning associated with these clouds. Caleb felt a raindrop splash on his arm, then another. He barely had the time to think *it's raining* before they were in a downpour. *Damn rain,* he thought. He'd had enough water today. Now they'd have to be soaked the whole way back. He surveyed the others, expecting frowns.

Ara had her eyes closed and face tilted skyward. Her arms were out at her sides, palms up. Ray and Connor were holding one another's hands and were spinning around each other in some kind of primeval square dance.

Caleb closed his eyes and let out a full breath of air through his nose. This was what the guy in the letters kept talking about.

He put his head back and faced the sky. He stuck out his tongue and drank in the warm beads of water.

O N THE JOURNEY BACK, a plan was formed for the next morning. They were going to meet at the creek, by the meadow, at eight a.m. Caleb told Ray he'd have to wear shoes this time. They'd also need food, water, and a shovel.

"I have a kid shovel at home," Ray said.

"Perfect." Caleb said his goodbyes and turned for home. The rain had all but stopped.

Mom was running up the path from their house. She slammed into the brothers and pulled them into her arms. "I was so worried," she said. "I saw all the smoke. And I couldn't find you."

"Sorry, Mom," Caleb said.

"Yeah, sorry, but we're okay," Connor said.

"Thank God for that." She let them go and looked at them. "It's times like this I almost wish you guys had cell phones."

The boys weren't allowed to have phones. Most of the kids at school had them, but their parents considered them a colossal waste of time. Caleb didn't mind, much. He was starting to feel the pressure to have a phone and be on social media like everyone else, but he still preferred the creek.

"Let's get back and get you guys some dinner," Mom said.

As they entered the house they heard the radio playing the news. "*...and stay there until further notice.*"

Mom jerked the plug of the radio from the wall.

"What was he talking about?" Caleb asked. "And why'd you unplug it?"

"Just some boring old news," Mom said, looking away. "What do you want for dinner?"

"Spaghetti please," Connor said without hesitation.

"Okay, you guys go get changed and I'll make it," Mom said, then bit her upper lip. She looked so sad.

They changed out of their wet clothes while their mom whipped up some spaghetti. The three of them sat down at the table to eat. Mom said a short blessing before they dug in, which was surprising; those were usually reserved for holiday meals. She didn't press them at all about where they were all day. Caleb was confused but relieved by that. He'd rather not have to lie to her unless it was absolutely necessary.

"Oh, I almost forgot," Mom said. "Your friend Nate called for you while you were out."

Caleb's posture bolted upright. "What'd he say?"

"He was wondering if you were home," she said. "I asked him how his mom, Amy, was doing, and he hung up on me."

"You know his mom?"

"Yes," said Mom. "We used to be best friends."

"What happened?" Connor said.

"Well." Mom paused, thinking. "We were friends throughout elementary and middle school. But once we hit high school, she started drinking a lot. I tried to not let it come between us, but it started to be too much. She was drinking heavily almost every day. She was getting into all kinds of trouble and became a very difficult person to be around. We remained friends, kind of. But it was never the same."

"So you ditched her?" Caleb said.

"Well, after high school I went off to college and she stayed here," Mom continued. "I tried to keep in touch, but we drifted apart. Then, when we were having babies at about the same time, I tried to rekindle the friendship. But the father of her child wouldn't allow her to speak with me." She rubbed the side of her face. "I hear he bailed on her and Nate after two or three years. I never reached out to her again. I probably should have. It's so sad really. She lives so close to me, and I haven't even seen her in years."

Caleb felt something he'd never associated with Nate before: pity. He didn't know about Nate's parents. Nate never talked about them at school. But no one really talked about his parents at school. You'd see most of them at football games and stuff though. But not Nate's parents. Thinking back, he realized he'd never even seen one of them.

"Have you guys considered what we talked about?" Mom said after several silent moments.

"About God?" Connor said.

"Yes," Mom said. "About accepting Jesus."

"I have," Caleb said.

"Me too," Connor said.

"And? Are you ready to do that?" The look on her face begged them to say yes.

"Yes." Caleb wasn't completely sure he responded this way because he meant it, or if he just wanted to oblige his pleading mother.

Connor nodded.

"Oh, I'm so glad," Mom said. "Will you follow me in a prayer?"

"Yeah," both boys affirmed.

She recited a prayer one line at a time. She waited for the boys to repeat each line before moving on to the next.

"Thank you, boys," Mom said when the prayer was over. "I love you so much." Tears formed in her eyes and a halfhearted smile crossed her lips. It seemed as if a weight was lifted from her shoulders. Not all of the weight; she still had a persistent bit of sadness in her face. But some of it had been washed away.

Caleb didn't feel any different. He wondered if he was supposed to.

His eyes wandered, then fixed on the big, canvas family portrait that hung on the wall in the dining area. It was a picture from around four years ago when they had taken a vacation to the Oregon coast. Mom and Dad each had one arm around the other, and the other arm holding one of the kids. Mom held Connor and Dad held Caleb. Haystack Rock shot up from the beach behind them while the ocean sparkled in the sun behind it.

They all looked so happy because, he thought, they genuinely were. This was before Dad lost his job, before Connor was burned, and before Mom was sick. Everything had been right with the world on that beach.

"That was a great vacation, wasn't it?" Mom said, noticing Caleb's stare.

"It was," Caleb said.

"I remember it like it was yesterday," Mom said with a sigh. "You guys had so much fun on that trip."

"That was the best vacation ever," Connor said. "Remember the crab pinched Dad's toe?"

"And the bumper cars."

"And the giant sand squid we made."

"And jumping into the waves all day," Caleb said. He could see himself: littler, laughing, and jumping into a wave for the first time. The ocean had been vast and scary to him the first time he'd been to the beach, when Connor was just a baby. He had nightmares about being lost at sea for years after that. But on that trip to Oregon he had jettisoned that fear. It was as if a switch went off in his head and he decided that fear wasn't going to control him. He was only ten years old. It didn't seem possible to him that a kid that age could do such things, but he clearly remembered it happening. He had an exact picture in his mind of everything around him in that moment. *But look at me now,* he thought. *I panic whenever anything goes wrong. Everything was easier before the accident, before I found out how brave I really am. Not at all.*

"You know what I'd like to do?" Mom said as they got up and put their dishes in the dishwasher.

"What?"

"Sit back, relax, and watch a movie with you guys," she said. "How about "The Fox and the Hound"? It was your favorite when you guys were that age." She pointed to the portrait. "And we haven't seen it in forever."

"Sounds good to me," Connor said.

"Sure." Caleb resisted kid's shows these days, but he was tired, and it really was his favorite movie once.

The kids flopped down on the couch on either side of their mom as she pulled a blue and green afghan over the three of them. Punky jumped up, like usual, and sat on Connor's lap.

A warm nostalgia coursed through Caleb as the movie opened. It chilled as he remembered the sad opening scene. The little fox losing his mother hit home with him now more than ever. He tightened his mouth and held back tears. His mom must have noticed. She put her arm around him and massaged his shoulder. Now the tears were imminent. The little green caterpillar's first appearance was the only thing that kept them at bay. A slight smile crossed his lips. He used to love that caterpillar.

It was nice sitting there with most of his family. He glanced at Connor from time to time and always found him enrapt with a smile on his face. His mom seemed to be enjoying being with them more than the movie; she watched the two of them at least as much as she watched the screen.

Tod, the fox, said, "Copper, you're my very best friend," followed by the famous line, "And we'll always be friends forever, won't we?" Caleb's thoughts turned to his friends. He didn't have a best friend. He used to have one: Jonathan. They were friends from day one of kindergarten through much of elementary school. Almost all of it; they had started to drift apart in the fourth grade. Jonathan was small, pale, and completely uninterested in sports. He and Caleb spent countless hours making comic books with these weird, alien-looking creatures. During recess at school, while everyone else was out playing soccer, the two of them played make-believe and imagined their next story.

The pull to join the others became palpable. Caleb had always been good at sports. Jonathan didn't stand a chance out there. The friendship fizzled. He felt bad, but what could he do? He lost interest in drawing comics, and he wanted to fit in with the sports playing group. He loved sports; that wasn't his fault.

When he saw Jonathan in the halls at middle school he'd say hi but that was about the extent of it now. Jonathan spent his summers in Baltimore with his dad. *Maybe I'll talk to him when he gets back?* He pondered the idea as the show played on.

When the movie reached its climax, and Copper stood between the hunter and Tod, the tears broke through. *If I only had that kind of courage*, Caleb thought. *That's how I should be. But I'm not. Not even close.*

He looked to the others, hoping that they didn't see him crying. They hadn't noticed. In fact, Mom was asleep, with her head on Connor's shoulder. Caleb discreetly wiped away the tears with the blanket.

Connor nudged Punky off of his lap and scooted out from the couch, while gently laying Mom down. She didn't wake. *She must have been exhausted from worrying.*

Chapter 13

THE BOYS WERE TIRED TOO, but not quite ready to hit the sack, so they slunk out to the backyard. It was a beautiful, warm night. Their dad had taught them the word for this scent: *petrichor* filled the twilit air. The clouds had all passed on, and the darkening sky was a theater of stars. Frogs chanted a rhythmic hymn in the background.

Caleb was staring off in the distance, lost in thought, when the back door slid open, making him jump. He turned around and saw his dad coming out. "Hey guys," he whispered. He gave them both hugs. "Whatcha doin'?"

"Not much," Caleb said. "We just got done watching "The Fox and the Hound." Mom fell asleep during it. Did you go to the fire?"

"Not this time," Dad said. "No one else showed up at the station. So I stood and watched as that cell came through and started the fire. Then watched it burn a bit before the rain seemed to have knocked it down. I've never seen a fire up here in the Cascades burn so hot and fast. Crazy." He shook his head. "Anyway, I felt like I should do something, so I took a rig and drove as close as I could around the perimeter. It looks like it burned most of the way up to the pond, er, lake, and a few acres past the river to the east. Another system is supposed to come through here and rain all night. No more thunderstorms though. Hopefully the rain can put it all the way out."

Connor looked like he was dying to tell their dad what happened to them. Caleb held up one finger to him, trying to indicate *one more day*. Connor must have understood well enough. He resisted telling, again.

"I got an idea," Dad said. "Wanna get our instruments and play a little?"

"Sure." Caleb was trying to learn the guitar, like his dad. But he was apprehensive about these jam sessions his dad would pressure him into from time to time. His dad was so much better than he was, and Caleb felt like he couldn't add anything to the music.

They all snuck in past Mom, grabbed their instruments, and came outside to sit around the dormant fire pit. Caleb and his dad had acoustic guitars, and Connor knew how to play three chords on his ukulele.

Caleb warmed up by playing the opening riff from "(Don't Fear) The Reaper."

"More cowbell," Dad said. He looked to the boys with an expectant expression. When he got nothing back but confused looks, he shrugged and started playing a basic blues progression.

The boys joined in. Caleb never listened to blues music, but he liked playing it. He could play the chords, and even mastered a few different turn-arounds. Connor's ukulele chords didn't really fit, but they were mostly drowned out by the guitars. Both boys had wide smiles.

The session built to a crescendo, then ended with a short solo from Dad.

"Nice job, boys," Dad said.

"Do one of your songs for us," Connor said.

"Okay. I do have a new one I was working on."

He started playing in a different style now, fingerpicking a beautiful melody. As he started singing, Caleb watched his fingers move over the fretboard. *How can he do such complicated playing while singing at the same time? I'll never be able to do that.* He didn't even hear the first verse of the song. He shook his head and paid attention to the chorus.

"So forgive me, but I haven't found God in a book," Dad sang. "I've found God in a look, from my sons when they laugh. As I look out on the ocean. In a forest path." There was a musical breakdown, followed by "Call me a dreamer, but I just can't rule out, the presence of magic beyond any doubt. There's more to life than we can know. Into adventure we go." He played a few more chords, then stopped. "Anyway, that's all I got for now."

"That was really good," Connor said.

"Thanks, but I'm not so sure."

"No, it was," Caleb said. "I don't know how you can do that."

"A lot of practice and time," Dad said. "But my lyrics could use some work. I've found out that writing songs isn't easy. It sounds so corny, now that I've heard it out loud."

"Why don't you believe in God?" Connor asked.

"Well…I kinda do," Dad said.

"But Mom said you weren't a Christian."

"Yeah, she's right about that."

"How can you 'kinda' believe in God?" Caleb said.

"That's a good question," Dad said. "I think that there is more to the universe than we can comprehend. There very well could be a higher power, or force that is overseeing it all. I'm just not sure."

"What about Jesus?" Connor said.

"You sound like your mom lately," Dad said with a smile. "But seriously, I like a lot of Jesus' teachings. I think if Christians actually followed what Jesus said, the world would be a much better place. At least America, anyway. But do I believe that he died for our sins and was resurrected three days later? No. I used to really want to believe that. But I just don't."

"Aren't you worried about hell?" Caleb said.

Dad paused for a moment. "Look up at the stars," he said. "That band across the sky is part of our galaxy, the Milky Way. If you were going the speed of light, it would take you over a hundred thousand years to get from one side of it to the other. And that is only one galaxy out of literally billions. I find it hard to believe that a god would make all of this, just so people on this

particular planet could confess their belief in something that happened in one specific place, and in one
specific time, or burn in hell for eternity."

"But what if he did?" Caleb said.

"Like Pascal's wager?"

"Huh?"

"Sorry. He was a philosopher from a long time ago,"
Dad said. "He said that all people are betting with their
eternal lives on whether or not God exists. If you bet
that he does, you're not risking anything really. But if
you bet that he doesn't exist, you're potentially risking
an eternal life in hell. So, he says, it makes much more
sense to believe he exists. But I got news for old Pascal:
belief isn't a decision."

"That was confusing," Connor said.

"Yeah, why isn't belief a decision?" Caleb said.

"What if I told you the sky was red?" Dad said.
"And everything you've ever known about color, and
the world really, was wrong. Could you believe that?"

"No," both boys said.

"Now what if your eternal soul was on the line.
And all you had to do was believe that it was red,
and you'd be saved. Could you make the decision to
believe it then?"

"No."

"This is a stupid analogy," Dad said. "But the point I'm feebly trying to make is that you can't *decide* to believe something. You can investigate something, and learn everything you can about it, but when it comes down to it, you either believe in it or you don't."

"It seems real to me," Connor said.

"Okay," Dad said. "I'm happy for you. And even a little jealous."

Connor's cheeks reddened.

"I'm not sure about it," Caleb said. "I want to believe it."

"It'd be okay if you did too," Dad said. "Your mother is a very smart woman and she believes. Her faith has been run through the gauntlet, and she came out on the other side as a believer."

"She had us say a prayer with her at dinner about accepting Jesus as our savior," Caleb said.

"Oh, good," Dad said. "That was important to her. I'm glad you guys did it. For her sake, at least."

"Is it weird being the only one who doesn't believe?" Caleb asked.

"Sometimes it is," Dad said. "I want to share this experience of life with you all, and sometimes I feel like I can't fully do that. Most of the people I associate with at work and stuff are Christians too, so I often feel like an outcast."

"I know how that feels," Connor said.

"I know you do, buddy." Dad reached out and gripped Connor's shoulder.

Caleb couldn't help but resent the bond they had in that moment. "I do too. I feel like, if I don't act a certain way at school, everyone judges me."

"I hear ya," Dad said. "I used to be so scared of being judged that I hid things from people too. I didn't get over it until I got older. Didn't start writing music until my thirties because I was terrified of what people would think. Even though I had wanted to before then. I'm still scared to share it with many people. But I want you guys to be more confident, more willing to be yourselves, regardless of what anyone may think." He made the little speech with his usual enthusiasm but at the end his lips tightened and he had a blank stare for a moment.

"Are you proud of me?" Caleb surprised himself by asking.

"Absolutely," Dad said, seeming to try his best to put on a happy face. "I'm proud of you all the time." Now he took hold of Caleb's shoulder. "But you know what shot into my head when you said that?"

"What?"

"It was Easter, you were six and Connor was three," Dad said. "We went to a park for a big Easter egg hunt. When it started, you bolted off and got a lot of eggs. When you came back, you saw your brother standing there holding an empty basket and crying. You didn't even hesitate. You walked right over to him and put a few eggs in his basket. I was so proud of you in that moment that my eyes teared up." He wiped his eye on his shirtsleeve. "They kind of are now, actually."

"What about me?" said Connor.

"Of course," Dad said. "I was so proud of you during your entire treatment and recovery after your burn. You were so brave during that time. And you're still brave every——"

"A frog!" Connor said, setting his ukulele on the wall of the fire pit, jumping out of his seat, and running toward the garden. He came back holding a big, greenish-brown frog with both hands. "It's the same one again. The one with the four spots!"

"I'm proud of that too," Dad said.

"What?" Connor said.

"You got so excited about that frog. I love that about you," Dad said.

A wide, contented smile crossed Connor's face. Caleb rolled his eyes, unintentionally.

"I love that about both of you," Dad said. "You guys have kept your sense of magic. Some kids your age have all but lost that. And most adults are missing it completely."

"Like Harry Potter?" Connor said.

"Yeah, kind of. Wouldn't you go to Hogwarts if you had the chance?" Dad said.

"Of course I would," Connor stated as the frog wriggled out of his grip.

"Yeah, me too," Dad said. "But what I really mean is that I want to keep my childlike sense of wonder about the world. And I don't want you guys to lose yours either."

"Okay, Dad," Caleb said.

"Goodbye, Frog," Connor said, waving as it hopped toward the woods.

Chapter 14

*C*ALEB AWOKE TO Connor's voice. Connor was shaking his shoulder and saying, "Wakey, wakey."

"What's up?"

"I woke up really early," Connor said. He was wearing the burn camp shirt from last year. It said, "Life's a Beach at Camp Tusbaye" in between two palm trees. "I can't wait to get out there."

Caleb looked around the room. The sun was up, but he didn't hear the usual cacophony of birds outside. "What time is it?"

"A little before seven, I think," Connor said.

"You must have hit your head in the river," Caleb said, reaching out and lightly rubbing a mark on his brother's forehead with his thumb. It was a red mark, slightly bigger than a quarter, just above his eyebrows.

"You too," Connor said, pointing to the same sort of spot on Caleb's forehead.

"Weird," Caleb said. "Well, let's get ready."

Caleb jumped out of bed and threw on some black basketball shorts and a dark green t-shirt with "Seaside, OR" written across the chest. He grabbed his empty back pack and put in the bear spray canister, the map, and the final clue. Then he went out in the kitchen and added four bottles of water, two apples, and an unopened box of Chicken in a Biscuit crackers. He saw a tape measure on the counter and he took that too. His parents were still in their room. *Should we go before they get up?* He wanted to get going, and he wasn't sure how long they'd stay asleep. He decided to write them a note.

Hey Mom and Dad,
Me and Conn are going on a hike today.
We'll be back later.
Hopefully with a big surprise for you!
Sorry we took off without saying bye.
Love, Me

He knew this would be letting the cat out of the bag in a way, but he was ready to let them know that he knew about Mom's sickness. If they couldn't get that gold today, they'd have to recruit Dad to help. Time was too precious for them to continue searching in vain.

But today…Today was going to be the day. He just knew it. Their parents would forgive them for leaving like this when they returned triumphantly with enough gold to erase all their worries.

The boys opened a box of Pop Tarts and ate them cold for breakfast as they left the house.

"Where're the chickens?" Connor said.

Caleb looked in the outside part of the coop. It was odd not to see them out eating at this time. "They must still be sleeping," he said. He checked the enclosed section of the coop. All of the chickens lay inside, not moving. He touched one and it was cold. Were they all dead? On any other day, this would have been upsetting. He considered them to be more like pets than just a source of eggs. But with everything going on, he didn't have time to question their deaths or to mourn. He firmly pushed it out of his mind and didn't mention it to his brother.

They rambled down the path to the creek with a bounce in their steps. Caleb could see the small figures of Ara and Ray up ahead waiting for them. His heart fluttered. He couldn't remember ever being this excited about anything.

"Guys," a voice called from behind them. It was their dad.

Oh no, Caleb thought. *Was he going to stop them from going before they even got a chance to start?* He turned around to see his dad running up the path.

"We were gonna tell you we were going, but you were still sleeping," Connor yelled to him.

"That's okay," Dad said as he approached. Then he stopped about ten yards away from them and closed his eyes tightly. A look of utter anguish came over his reddening face. He put both hands on top of his head, obscuring his mask of pain with his elbows.

The boys rushed to him. "What's wrong?" Caleb said. "Is Mom okay?"

Dad took in three deep breaths and let them out slowly. "Yes, Mom's okay," he whispered.

He uncovered his face and put an arm around each of his sons. His cheeks were wet. Caleb noticed that Dad had the same sort of mark on his head that he and Connor did.

"Did you bump your head too?" Caleb said.

"What?" Dad said. "Oh, I mean, yeah, I must have."
He looked to the right, his eyes blinking rapidly, his
fists clenched, and took in a lung-expanding breath
through his nose. He blew it out through pursed lips.
"Please come back and see your mom."

"Okay, but we have something very important to
do this morning," Caleb said, dropping his backpack
beside the path. "Just a sec," he called to Ara and Ray.

"We just want to spend a little time with you, then
you can go," Dad said.

The boys walked back toward the house under
Dad's arms.

As they neared the yard, their mom appeared
on the path wearing a long t-shirt and pajama pants.
When she got close to them she dropped down to her
knees in the dirt. Caleb didn't get a good look at her
face because she immediately curled down and hugged
her knees. He could hear her crying. He'd heard her
cry many times before, but this was the most raw,
uncontrolled crying he'd ever heard from her. Both
boys knelt beside her and enveloped her in their arms.
How long they stayed like this, Caleb didn't know. Tears
formed in his eyes and he let out a few sobs. He hated
to see his mom like this. He heard Connor crying too.
Dad knelt down and rubbed the back of Mom's neck.

"It's gonna be okay, Mom," Connor said after his tears had passed. "We know about your cancer. And we know how we can help."

Caleb felt a weight lift from his chest. *No more secrets*, he thought. *I wanted to surprise them with the treasure, but this is too much. I'm glad it's out now.*

Mom took a few moments to pick her head up and look at them. She was beautiful just then, despite the tear-streaked face and messy hair. She had the same kind of mark on her forehead that they all did. *Weird*, Caleb thought. She gave Dad a confused look. Caleb didn't see what his dad's reaction to the look was.

"You know?" Mom said.

"Yes," Connor said. "We overheard you guys talking the other night. Sorry about sneaking and listening to you, but we were worried that something scary was going on. So we heard about how you have cancer and how we don't have enough money for the doctors."

"But we're gonna save you, Mom!" Caleb said, jumping up. "We found pieces of a treasure map. A real one. And we're gonna go get a bunch of gold. Today! It will be enough to get you the treatment you need, I just know it."

Both parents started crying again. It was impossible to tell if they were tears of pain or joy.

When Dad regained composure, he said, "That's great, guys. That gold will be exactly what we need. I can't believe it. I should have known that our awesome boys would come to the rescue."

"Do you want to come with us?" Connor said.

"I really do," Dad said. "But I'd better stay here with your mom."

Mom and Connor stood up together and held each other close. Dad took Caleb by the shoulder and walked toward the house a few paces.

"You know I'm so proud of you, Caleb," Dad said.

Warmth coursed through Caleb's chest. In that instant, all else faded away, and making his dad proud meant everything to him.

"I love you more than life itself," Dad said, pulling him close.

"I love you too, Dad."

"You go out there today and have the time of your life. You hear me?"

"Yes."

"I mean it," Dad said. "Have an epic adventure. And kiss that girl that's out there waiting——"

"Dad!" Caleb's face turned deep red.

"Why not?" Dad said, trying to smile. He stepped back and gripped Caleb's shoulder. "Okay, go say good——" his lips tightened so hard they turned pale. "Go talk to your mom."

Caleb and Connor crossed paths as they each went to the other parent. His mom hadn't stopped crying, apparently. He went right up to her and held her close.

"You mean everything to me, Caleb," Mom sobbed. "Every day I thank God for giving me the two best boys I could have ever asked for."

Caleb didn't know what to say.

"I love you so much," Mom said.

"I love you too, Mom."

"Until we meet again, may God hold you in the palm of His hand."

Caleb was confused by what she said and all the outpouring of affection lately, but chose to say nothing. Instead, he opted to hold her tighter.

They stayed huddled together. Eventually Connor and Dad came over to them and formed a group hug.

The four of them remained in the embrace for a long time.

Chapter 15

ALEB LOOKED OVER HIS SHOULDER as he and his brother walked back down the path. His parents were sitting in the dirt, together. He felt as if he'd been blindsided by a storm of emotion. He hated to see them so sad, so fragile. But he was invigorated by the idea that he could change that. He and his brother could fix everything. He looked over at Connor, saw him dealing with what just happened to them, and also saw the excitement and the determination to prevail over it all on his face. He'd never felt closer to his brother.

They reached the creek and met up with the others. Ray had worn shoes. Actually big rubber rain boots. He had brought a three-foot-long shovel with a handle on the end. Ara had her school backpack strapped to her back. Caleb noticed that Ara had the same strange marking on her head that everyone else had. Ray seemed to be the only one that didn't have it. That was very odd, but would have to remain a mystery. They had big things to do today.

"Jeez, took you long enough," Ray said, jumping on Connor's back. "Let's get to the lake and find that treasure!"

"Sorry," Connor said, while trying to shake him off. "We had to have a little talk with our parents this morning."

"We snuck out," Ray said.

"Yeah," Ara said. "Our parents told us we couldn't leave the house today."

"Aren't you gonna get in trouble?" Connor asked.

"Oh yeah," Ara said. "But the thought of missing out on this scared me more than the punishment we're gonna get."

"Our parents were crying when we left," Connor said.

"Yeah," said Caleb. "We told them about the gold. And our dad said it's exactly what they need. Our mom was very emotional this morning, but we know she'll be okay if we can find it."

"For Amber Greene then," Ara said, putting her hand in the air toward the boys.

"Yeah, for her." Ray touched his sister's hand from Connor's back.

"For Mom," the boys said, clasping hands with everyone in the middle.

A few days ago, Caleb would have thought this was the corniest thing he'd ever seen. But now, he saw it as an act of solidarity with his brother, and with these two friends who had become so important to him in such a small amount of time.

If Nate saw them clasping hands he would laugh and humiliate them. Caleb, remembering his classmate, scanned the area for any sign of him. He hadn't seen Nate since that night on the hill. That fact, along with the fact that he had called their house yesterday, worried the hell out of Caleb. It wasn't like Nate to forget something like money. They were too close to it now; they couldn't let him screw everything up.

"Let's be quiet as we start up the trail," Caleb whispered. "Everyone needs to be extra careful that we're not being followed."

"By who?" Ray said.

"Nate Pearson."

"That jerk knows about the treasure?" Ara said.

"Yes," Caleb said. "He followed us when we found one of the clues. He says he wants it for himself."

"Let's get going," Ara said. "I have an idea."

After a final look around, the group started up the trail in silence. After about a hundred yards, Ara put one finger up to her mouth, slipped away off of the path, and hid behind a large Douglas fir. Caleb understood her idea and kept hiking, the younger ones following his lead.

Their pace slowed, subconsciously making it easier for Ara to catch up after her vigil. For the first time in a while, Caleb noticed the world around him. It was absolutely beautiful.

Beams of sunlight broke through between the trees and illuminated the lush, green ferns on the forest floor. An almost invisible mist hung in the air, reflecting the shards of light so that they appeared to be streams from heaven. The still air was warm, not hot like it was the day before. It was the perfect temperature, he thought. And the forest was silent this morning.

His reverie was interrupted by the sound of footfalls coming up from behind. Ara had run to catch back up to them. "I waited for, like, ten minutes, and I didn't hear or see anything."

"Okay, good," Caleb said, his biggest worry about this trip alleviated.

The walk up to Skydiver Hill was uneventful. Everyone was either hypnotized by the forest's beauty or quietly contemplating their destination.

A short time after the transition was made to the other trail, they ran into the burned area. The scenery went from beautiful to bleak in an instant. The fire had torched almost everything on the ground. It had burned so fast, however, that it didn't get into the tops of the trees. So the sun was still blocked out by the dense canopy above. The lower parts of the trunks were singed black. A powdery, gray ash was all that remained of most of the dense underbrush they had fought through the day before. Scattered throughout the eerie landscape were hot spots that issued a thin layer of smoke, which hung in the air like fog. A few pockets of unburned brush still gave off an orange glow as they smoldered.

"It smells like a campfire," Ray said.

"Yeah," Connor said. "But not in a good way. It's too much."

Every footstep sent puffs of fine ash in the air. Before long, the four of them were coughing up a storm.

"Our dad said that it burned most of the way up to the lake," Caleb said.

"That sucks," Ara said, covering a sneeze in the crook of her elbow.

The fire had completely erased the path. Getting bearings in this desolate landscape wasn't easy, but Caleb knew which way north was, and he knew they'd make it if they kept going that way.

They hiked and hiked through the barren wasteland. It seemed to be taking hours. No one talked. They all kept their heads down and lips closed to avoid mouths caked with ash. They followed Caleb single file.

They approached the downslope of a hill and through a sparse area of the canopy, they could see the lake at the bottom. The underbrush slowly reappeared. At first it was charred black. As they walked down the hill, the brush became less and less charred, until they made it back to unburned forest.

Caleb started to jog. They were so close now that excitement buzzed throughout his body. He angled his approach to arrive at the west bank of the lake. The X on the map was north of the lake, and that would be the fastest way around. They were all running now, and in no time they had reached the gold's approximate location on the map.

"We made it," Connor said, panting.

"Now let's find that final tube," Ara said, already searching the treetops.

Chapter 16

*C*ALEB HAD A SINKING FEELING. He wasn't sure how he didn't think of this before. "We've got a problem, guys," he said.

"What is it?" Connor said.

"That letter was written over a hundred years ago," Caleb said. "So the tree we're looking for would have grown a lot, and maybe even died, since that tube was placed. How can we possibly follow the precise instructions from the poem?"

"It depends on how old the tree was when that guy put the tube there," Ara said. "Trees kind of stop growing upwards eventually. They just get bigger trunks every year. It also depends on what kind of tree it was. So don't give up hope yet."

"How do you know that?" Connor said.

"I love plants and nature," she said. "I want to be a botanist someday. That or a Claymation animator."

"Okay, I hope you're right," Caleb said, getting the map from his backpack. "So you're saying it's gonna be a huge tree then?"

"Yeah, it should be."

They all gathered around to see if they could pinpoint the location of the tree on the map. They needed to head east. They spread out in an informal grid and swept the lake's edge while inspecting every part of every tree.

Caleb glanced ahead and saw an enormous oak. Something inside him told him that it was the tree. He hurried past the other trees, only looking up occasionally. When he got to the oak, he craned his neck back and examined every branch of the giant. He heard a splash in the lake. He glanced over to see ripples in the water, but no indication of what had made them. When he looked back up he immediately saw it.

There, nestled in the crook of a limb, was the final tube. It was about twenty feet up, and another ten feet out from the massive trunk.

"Over here," Caleb called. "I found it!"

Caleb assessed the tree for a climbable route as the others rushed over to him. Connor and Ray began jumping up and down, giddy with excitement. Ara's smile reached out across her entire face. It was the most beautiful thing Caleb thought he'd ever seen. He caught himself staring at her, but looked away before she noticed.

Connor got the final clue out of Caleb's backpack, and he and Ara studied it while Caleb looked over the tree.

"How can we get up there?" Ray said.

"I think we'll have to boost you up to the lowest branch there," Caleb said, pointing. "And you can climb the rest of the way and then shimmy out on that big branch."

"Yes!" Ray rocked back and forth, a permanent grin glued to his face.

"Can you guys help him get up and stand on my shoulders?"

Connor and Ara began to lift Ray up on Caleb's back. "Hold on a sec," Caleb said. "Here, drop this down through the tube when you get up there." He pulled his lucky rock from his pocket and handed it to Ray.

Ray was a wiry kid; he made it up from Caleb's shoulders and was shimmying out in no time.

"Cuidado," Ara shouted to him.

"I know, I know."

He reached his target, fished the rock from his pocket, kissed it, and dropped it down through the tube. It plunked on the soft dirt of the forest floor with a small, dull thud.

"Here's the nearest birch tree." Connor had walked about thirty feet to the only birch in the area.

Caleb retrieved the measuring tape from his pack, walked to his brother, and handed him the end. He extended the tape as he made his way back to the lucky rock.

"Okay, so now we have a line," Caleb said. "That's right, right?"

"I think so," Ara said. "So now we have to follow that line for fifty feet from the rock."

"That way, right?" Caleb pointed in the direction going away from the birch tree.

"Yes."

Caleb marched out exactly fifty feet and made a mark in the dirt with his shoe. *Could there really be gold under my feet?* Feelings of doubt invaded his mind. He had come all this way believing in the treasure's existence, but now that they were here, the idea seemed absurd.

Ray, who had climbed down with the help of his sister, held his shovel above his head and shook it up and down like a miniature Tusken Raider. "Time to dig!"

He began digging on the spot that Caleb had marked. The others stood around him and watched.

"Like government work," Connor said.

"Yeah." Caleb gave a nervous chuckle. He didn't ever understand, but it was something their dad would often say in situations like this.

As he watched Ray dig, Caleb thought, *There's no way this is the right spot. That tree would have grown a lot. There can't really be gold down there anyway. This whole thing is crazy. And too good to be true. If something sounds too good to be true, it's because it is*, he thought, echoing something he'd heard at school or on TV.

"Somebody else wanna dig?" Ray said, panting.

"I will." Connor jumped forward, took the shovel, and started where Ray had left off.

The four of them took turns digging. By Connor's second turn, they had dug about four feet underground. Caleb's fears were being confirmed. There was nothing here.

Connor leaped into the hole and thrust the shovel in the ground. A loud thump reverberated through the woods. Caleb's hands instinctively clapped together in front of his face, as if he was praying. Ara was wringing her hands and staring at Connor. Ray was running in place.

Connor took a few more digs from different angles and yelled, "A box! A big box!"

Everyone crowded into the hole and dug around the box with their hands. When the top was uncovered, they tried lifting it out. It was far too heavy. They couldn't budge it. Caleb took the shovel and wedged it under the box's cover. He pried it sideways, but that wasn't enough force to move the cover. He quickly dug an offshoot little trench beside the box. He wedged the shovel under the cover again, with the handle sticking out over the trench. Pushing down with all of his strength was still not enough to dislodge the covering.

Connor repositioned himself and helped push the handle down. Ara and Ray did the same. They were all pushing down with all their might. The shovel gave way and fell in the trench. The cover of the box had been lifted up about two inches. Caleb stood over the box, grabbed the top, and wrenched at it with forceful tugs. The lid came off in Caleb's hands as he fell backwards on his butt. He jumped up and peered inside.

CHAPTER 16

There was a burlap sack covering the contents of the box. On top of that was placed another piece of inscribed parchment. Connor grabbed the parchment with one hand, and ripped the burlap sack off with the other.

And there it was.

Jagged, golden rocks, about the size of a man's fist, filled the entire box. They caught the sunlight and almost seemed to sparkle. Caleb guessed there were at least thirty of them.

No one said a word. They all stared in awe at what they had found. Caleb only realized he'd been holding his breath when his lungs started to ache. He reached down and picked one of the nuggets up. It was heavy, but maybe a little lighter than he expected. He turned it over in his hands. *This is real*, he thought. *We really did it.*

He noticed that the others all had a rock in their hands as well. They all contemplated the gold in silence. The shock and realization of it all was apparently too much for words to express.

"Bravo," a voice called from the east.

Nate Pearson came out from a stand of trees, clapping with his hands up by his head.

Chapter 17

"WHY'D YOU DO THIS without me, Caleb?" Nate said, a mixture of anger and pain on his face. He had the same mark that they all had on his forehead too. But no one had a chance to wonder about that.

The gold tumbled from Caleb's hand, landing near his foot.

"You said you wouldn't do this without me, Caleb." Nate threw a rock he'd been holding against the old oak tree. "I thought we were friends. But you and your lame little gang here decided to sneak around and do it without me. Well I don't need you. This gold is mine. All of it. And there ain't nothing any of you are going to do about it."

Caleb felt the familiar paralyzing panic spread from his chest down to his feet. His jaw clenched. His vision blurred as his pulse pounded in his temples.

"How'd you find us?" Ara said.

"Let's get to the lake and find that treasure," Nate said in a high-pitched voice, imitating Ray from earlier that day. "Sound familiar? I knew something was up, so I was coming to see my old buddy Caleb when I saw you two cholos standing by the creek. After I heard the thing about the lake I came straight here and waited for your dumb asses. I knew there wasn't a real lake around here so I figured this pond is what you idiots meant."

"You can't have this gold," Connor said, confidence radiated from his eyes.

"What?"

"We need it." Connor stared at him. "It's ours."

Events moved in slow motion as Caleb stood and watched. Nate approached Connor and grabbed the gold nugget out of his hand. He stood directly in front of him, looking down. He was a full two heads higher than his brother. Connor glared up at him in defiance.

"Ha ha, what are you gonna do?" Nate said.

"Give it back." Connor reached for the gold.

Nate pushed him back with one hand. Connor stepped forward and swung a wild haymaker with his right fist. It connected with Nate's ear. Nate howled in pain. A look of hatred covered his face. He dropped the rock and clenched his hand.

"I don't care if he is a burn victim, that little shit is not gonna punch me," he said as he swung his fist around, connecting with Connor's jaw and knocking him to the ground.

He pulled his foot back, preparing to kick Connor in the face while he was down.

"Stop!" Caleb roared.

Nate stopped and looked up.

Caleb ran over to his brother, helped him up, and then stood in front of him.

"You don't ever touch him again!" he said, glaring into Nate's eyes.

"What, I'm supposed to be scared of you?"

"If you ever mess with my brother again, you'd better be."

The two stared at each other, unmoving.

"You are done at school," Nate said. "You're not gonna have a friend in the world. And you won't play football ever again."

"I don't care."

"Just get out of here," Nate said. "I need this gold, and I'll knock your ass out too if I have to."

"It's not yours, it's ours."

"Seriously, take your friends, and your ugly, burnt little—"

Caleb rushed forward and smashed Nate in the nose. Blood instantly gushed down his face and onto his shirt. Nate swung back at him with his left hand, but Caleb leaned back and dodged it. Caleb cocked back and put everything he had into a right hook that sent Nate sprawling to the ground. He jumped down to his knees and rolled Nate over to his back. He intended to pound him into the dirt, to not stop until he was unconscious, and maybe not even stop then.

"Okay, okay," Nate said, his hands guarding his face. There was something so pathetic about his tone that Caleb paused.

Nate covered his bloody face with his hands and began sobbing.

Caleb stood up. For the first time, he noticed that his hand throbbed with pain. He wondered if he'd broken it, but he didn't care if he had. Adrenaline still pumped through his body.

"He's a burn *survivor*," Caleb said, standing over Nate, almost yelling the last word.

He looked to Connor. His brother's cheek was red and starting to puff up, but he had a huge grin across his face. The two of them stepped toward each other and embraced. Caleb had never felt so good in his entire life. He felt a connection with his brother that he thought he'd never have. Tears filled his eyes.

Through the tears he could see Ara, who had been holding Ray during the confrontation, approaching them. He hid his face in Connor's shoulder. She stood back and let them have a moment. When they let go of each other she said, "I'm sorry he was so mean to you, Connor."

"What, this?" He pointed to his puffed up cheek.

"I mean the nasty stuff he said."

"He wasn't the first, and he won't be the last," Connor said. "There will always be jerks in the world. But it's their problem, not mine."

"Exactly," Caleb said.

"I'll just stick with the good people, like you guys." Connor smiled.

Ray gave Connor a high five and the two of them ran over to the box.

"You did great," Ara said. She was looking down, but shot several glances up at Caleb. One hand was twirling her hair, and the other was tucked across her chest and under her arm.

"Thanks," Caleb said. The thrill of victory had his confidence at an all-time high. He thought, *Is this the moment? Should I kiss her?* His heart barely had time to slow down after the fight, now it resumed top speed. Her eyes met his, and he looked into them as he stepped forward. She looked down again, then back up. Both of her arms fell down to her sides. He paused, confused by her body language. He looked away. His face felt hot.

"You guys," Connor called, "come read this last note. It's really nice."

The moment had passed. Caleb was embarrassed, but he didn't let it get him down. He was feeling awesome. There would be other chances; he just knew it.

For now, he was going to enjoy this string of victories. The gold actually existed. And they'd found it, by themselves. His mom was going to be able to get the treatment she needed. He'd overcome his problem with freezing up in emergencies and he felt like that might be for good. A new confidence had him holding his head up high. He beat the crap out of Nate Pearson, something he would have never thought he was capable of doing. And he and his brother were united, and that felt the best out of it all.

Chapter 18

CALEB STROLLED OVER to the box of gold with Ara. Connor handed him the last note. He held it so Ara could see and read it aloud:

12th June, 1859

My two boys.

You made it to the end.
    Words can't tell how proud I am of you.
    You guys did this, together.
    The bond between you two is so important. You are brothers in more than name. I see that all the time.

I know there's been ups and downs. I know there's been fights. And at times you haven't wanted to be around each other.

But here you are.

Successful treasure hunters.

I hope I ended up having enough time to make this a 2 or 3 clue, proper treasure hunt. That's my plan, as of now. Either way, nice work in findin this! Spend it wisely. Use it to improve our family's lives. Your Momma's life. But also use it to make the world a better place.

If I'm with you right now (I hope I am), then turn around and shoot me a smile. That has always been, and will always be enough for me.

If I'm not with you, send a smile skyward.

You two are the greatest joys of my life, your Momma's too. We love you more than you could know.

If I never get the privilege of seeing you again in this life, I hope I will see you someday in whatever is next.

Love Always,
Dad

"Yeah, that was nice," Caleb said. He looked up into the clear, blue sky and smiled. Every time he read these old letters, especially this one, he got goosebumps on his arms and had the strange feeling that they were somehow meant for him and Connor.

"I wish he would have made it back to his kids." Connor rolled a piece of gold between his hands.

"I hear ya," Caleb said. "But at least we'll be able to spend it wisely, like he wrote."

"We should look up these people's names on the internet or something." Connor tossed the gold up and caught it.

"We haven't had the internet all summer." Caleb pulled the box of crackers from his bag, grabbed a handful, and passed it on.

"We do," said Ray. "But our parents locked it."

"I bet they'd let us use it for something like that though," Ara said, munching a mouthful of crackers.

"Cool, we should check it out some time." Caleb knelt down and began placing gold nuggets into his backpack. He tested the weight, then put in a few more. He settled on carrying fifteen of them.

Connor put a golden rock in each pocket, and carried one in each hand. Ray struggled to grip them, so he put one nugget back in the box and carried one in both of his hands. Ara loaded the rest into her backpack.

"Ready?" Caleb said.

They began hiking west together.

"I'm sorry about what I said, Connor," Nate called, still sitting in the dirt in the place he had been subdued.

Connor paused, then turned around. "Apology accepted."

"I'm such a piece of shit," Nate said, laying his head down into his hands.

The four friends stood, watching him, not knowing what to say.

Caleb thought, *Yeah, you are a piece of shit.*

"My mom," Nate mumbled. Then looked up and said, "I wanted to help my mom."

"How?"

"I don't know," Nate said. "But she needs help. Maybe a rehab place or something."

"Rehab?"

"I think she's dying. She never leaves the house, and she's hooked on liquor and drugs." A grimace of pain engulfed his face and he buried it between his knees.

Connor walked over to him. He looked down at Nate as he cried. The two gold nuggets he'd been carrying fell to the dirt in front of him. Nate looked up with bloodshot eyes and was overcome with emotion. He hid his face in his legs again, and wrapped his arms around his knees.

Connor went back to the others. Caleb put an arm around him as they started back down around the lake. Caleb envied his brother's capacity for compassion. But not in the same way that he used to envy him for all of the attention that he got. This felt more like simple respect, and an internal challenge to try to emulate that compassion. The idea of copying Connor in anything was a foreign one. But it didn't repulse him.

Weird, he thought, and smiled to himself.

Chapter 19

"How much money in gold do you think we have?" Ray asked the group.

"I asked Dad the other day how much a pound of gold was worth," Connor said.

Caleb shot him a look of playful disbelief.

"What?" said Connor. "I was really sneaky about it." He chuckled. "Anyway, he told me he thought it was like $15,000 per pound or something."

"So how many pounds do we have?" Ray said.

"I don't know." Caleb stopped. "How much do you weigh?"

"Uh, I think I weigh like fifty pounds."

Caleb dropped his backpack and lifted Ray up with both hands. He moved him up and down, trying to get a good feel for his weight. Then he put him down, picked up his pack, and did the same thing with it. "I'd guess this weighs about twenty-five pounds or so."

"So then I probably got ten or fifteen in my bag," Ara said as they continued their hike.

"So if we add a few pounds for the other ones, we have maybe forty-five pounds," Caleb said.

Ara's eyes pointed up as she mumbled to herself. "So that's $675,000 worth of gold then!"

Caleb looked confused.

"What?" Ara said. "I like math too."

"That's over half a million dollars!" Connor's eyes were wide.

"How much is a doctor for your mama?" Ray said.

"I have no idea," said Caleb. "But it can't be that much. We'll probably have a ton left over."

They had come up the slope from the lake and were now trudging through the burned forest again.

"What are you gonna do with your part, Ara?" Connor asked.

"Well, we'll see if that really will be enough for your mom first." Ara rubbed her chin. "But...if I did get some, I'd probably take my family to Disneyland. I've never been there before. I'd like to go during Halloween because the Haunted Mansion has a Nightmare Before

Christmas theme and the whole park gets decorated. You guys should come too."

"That'd be awesome," Connor said.

"I'm still getting a bracelet for Mama, a hat for Papa, a bike for me, and a pretty quinceñera dress for my sister," Ray said.

"I've still got a little over a year to go before my quinceñera."

"Okay, just a pretty dress then."

Ara laughed. "Thank you, Ramón."

"Ramón?"

"Yeah, yeah, that's my real name," Ray said. "They named me after some singer. But I like Ray better."

They were tasting soot in their mouths now, so they all stopped talking and glided toward home. They were weighed down with gold, but their feet seemed lighter on the trip back. In what seemed like no time to Caleb, they were past the burned area and arriving at Skydiver Hill. They made the transition to the other trail and continued at a power walker's pace.

"Hey Caleb," called Ray from the back of their single file line, "What will you do if you have any extra money?"

Caleb turned his head to the side and spoke loudly so Ray could hear him as they walked. "I was thinking about that letter. About how he told those kids they should use it to make the world a better place. So I think I want to donate some of it to the families of cancer patients. Not everyone falls into a buried treasure hunt just at the right time. Maybe that or cancer re——"

There was a loud snarling sound, and then Ray screamed from behind them.

Caleb swung around to see a wolf on the trail with Ray's booted foot in its mouth. The wolf was attempting to drag him into the trees. Ray, who had been knocked to the ground and was lying prone, scratched at the ground, trying to find a handhold.

"Ray!" Ara cried as she ran toward him.

The wolf looked at her with one eye and gave such a vicious growl that she stopped in her tracks.

Caleb saw this was the same wolf that nearly attacked Connor days ago. It still favored its right front paw, and it was still very skinny. Its left eye was swollen shut and caked with dried blood.

He flipped off his backpack and retrieved the bear spray. He disengaged the safety as he crept toward the hungry wolf. He motioned for Connor and Ara to move back. The wolf kept his eye on Caleb's approach, but continued to drag Ray off of the trail. Its snarling was unsettling, and much louder than Caleb had thought possible. Ray's face mirrored pure panic and he was hyperventilating.

When Caleb figured he was close enough, he stopped and aimed the nozzle. "Close your eyes, Ray." He pulled the trigger, but nothing happened. He squeezed harder; still nothing. He examined the trigger mechanism, but couldn't see what was making it malfunction. He tried again. And again.

The wolf let go of the boot and positioned himself over the top of Ray's little frame. It bellowed an awful noise that sounded more like a roar than a bark. Caleb stepped back.

"I'm going to try and distract it," Ara said in a whisper, as if the wolf could understand her. "When I draw it away, grab my brother."

Ara circled around to the other side of the wolf, giving it a wide berth. Its one good eye followed her every movement. When she was back on the trail to the north she began shouting in Spanish and waving her arms. The wolf took an even more aggressive stance, but it didn't budge. It remained standing over its prey, unwilling to give up the meal it so desperately needed. Saliva dripped from its jowls and splashed on Ray's cheek.

Ara stopped. "I have an idea," she yelled.

She turned around and ran up the trail.

The wolf, overcome by the ingrained instinct to hunt, took off after her.

Caleb knew he had to act fast. He ran to Ray, grabbed him under his armpits, and dragged him backwards. At the same time he saw that the wolf was closing on Ara. Caleb dropped Ray, cupped his hands around his mouth, and shouted louder than he'd ever shouted before. Connor followed his lead.

The wolf turned around. It looked at Ray, who was still lying on the ground, and sprinted back toward him. Caleb had almost no time to think. He jumped down and covered Ray with his body. He braced himself for a flesh tearing bite.

A high-pitched yelp pierced the air.

Caleb looked up to see the wolf laying on its side, and Connor holding Caleb's backpack. The wolf struggled to get back to its feet. Connor strode toward it and drew back the weighted pack. He swung it like a golf club and smashed it into the wolf's muzzle. It let out another loud yelp, scrambled to its feet, and limped away into the woods.

The three older kids instinctively circled Ray and watched the tree line for several moments.

When it was apparent that the wolf was not returning, Ara crouched down and checked out her brother. "Are you okay?"

"Yeah," said Ray, "I think I am."

He was still visibly shaken, but somehow seemed to be unhurt. She took off his rubber boot and examined his foot and ankle. There were no puncture wounds, just some redness and some slight swelling.

"Oh, I was so scared," Ara said.

"You were scared?" Ray said. "I think I peed myself."

They all let out nervous chuckles, relieved that the ordeal was over, but still in shock and saturated with adrenaline.

Chapter 20

"ARE YOU SURE THAT wolf didn't scratch your head?" Ara asked her brother. "You've got that same little mark that we all do now."

Ray rubbed his forehead. "I don't think so. It doesn't hurt or anything." It didn't seem important just now.

They made the rest of the trek back to the creek without much talking. They all were hyper-aware of their surroundings now. They scanned the tree line and made multiple checks over their shoulders. Ray limped for the first hundred yards or so, then realized that he really wasn't in any pain.

The mood of the group returned to jovial remarkably fast, considering the amount of danger they'd just been in.

Caleb was starting to feel sleepy. The sun's position told him that it was probably only about seven o'clock, but they had had one hell of a day, so he understood the tiredness.

"Aaah, the creek," Connor said, cupping its cool water in his hands and splashing it into his face.

Ray jumped into the creek boots first, soaking Connor with his splash. Connor laughed and threw water back at him. Caleb dropped his pack, shrugged at Ara, and tackled Connor into the creek. His momentum sent him flying over the top of his brother and into the water beside him. They both broke into laughter as they stood up and splashed each other. Ara leaped in and joined the fun.

They returned to the bank minutes later, soaked, with jaws that were sore from smiling and laughing.

"I'm starving," Ray said, rubbing his belly. "Are you guys?"

"Not really," Ara and Connor said in unison. Then they both said, "Jinx" at the same time and giggled.

It seemed odd, considering all they'd done and how little they'd eaten today, but Caleb wasn't hungry either.

"I'm gonna go home and get some food," Ray said, handing his lump of gold to Caleb. "You coming Ara?"

"In a few minutes," she said. "I was hoping to dry off a little before walking back."

Caleb's heart fluttered as an idea popped into his head. "Maybe Connor could walk you home?"

"Uh, yeah, I could do that," Connor said, wringing out his shirt.

"I'll wait for you here," Caleb said. "And when you get back we'll go tell Mom the good news."

"Okay, be right back."

The two of them headed toward the Flores house, almost skipping down the path together.

"Good job today, Ray," Caleb called. "With everything. You're one tough kid!"

"Thank you," Ray called back. "This was the best day ever. Life is good, amigo. See you in the next one."

Caleb looked confused by the comment.

"My Papa says that sometimes instead of 'see you tomorrow'," Ara said, shrugging. "He's still learning English."

"Oh, okay."

They stood in silence for a moment. Caleb fidgeted with his lucky rock and shot glances at Ara. She twirled the hair from her temple and stared at the running water.

"Thank you for jumping on my brother and covering him," Ara said, eyes still pointing away. "I did see that." She looked over at him.

"I didn't know what else to do."

"Well it was brave."

"Thanks," Caleb said. But he thought, *I'm not that brave. If I was I'd kiss you right now.* Dad's advice echoed through his mind. Part of his brain fought against it, fearing the embarrassment of rejection. Another part made a decision.

As he stepped forward he felt like he wasn't in command of his body. He put a hand on Ara's waist and slowly moved his head toward hers. She didn't flinch. In fact, he thought she might have moved toward him slightly. Their lips touched, only for a moment, then he stepped back. Her face had reddened, but there was a grin across it. Caleb's chest felt light and his legs felt wobbly. He smiled back at her.

He took her hand, led her across the creek at the island, and up to the meadow where it sloped down toward the stream. They sat down together on the grass and listened to the creek go by. Caleb wondered if the creek's soothing sound did as much for her as it did for him. He wondered what she was thinking.

Caleb yawned. He turned away from Ara, not wanting her to think he was bored. That wasn't even close to being the case, but he was getting more and more tired.

He wasn't sure how much time had passed when he saw Connor jogging up the path toward them. He jumped up. Ara stood as well, and the two of them walked back across the creek.

"Thank you for helping to save my brother today, Connor," Ara said.

"You're welcome." Connor yawned.

Caleb and Ara shared his infectious yawn.

"Oh man, I'm tired," Ara said. "I'm gonna get back and go to bed." She gave Connor a high five, then turned around and gave Caleb a hug. "See you in the next one," she said in his ear.

He hugged her back. "Yeah, see you in the next one."

She dropped her backpack and walked down the path toward her house, turning to wave twice before disappearing around a bend.

Chapter 21

"YOU WANNA SIT BY THE creek a minute before we go tell them everything?" Caleb said. He felt like he needed to take a breath before entering into the emotional scene that was about to happen at their house. He was eager to get home, but wanted to say something to Connor first. He just wasn't sure what he wanted to say yet.

"Sure," Connor said.

They jumped over the creek via the usual route and took seats next to each other in the tall grass.

Caleb had so much he wanted to say, but he didn't know where to start. Connor spoke first. "Thanks for sticking up for me," he said.

"It's something I should have done a long time ago."

"Well, like Mom says, better late than never."

"Yeah, I guess so," Caleb said. "But I'm still sorry I didn't do it earlier."

"It's okay."

"I'm sorry about a lot of things."

Connor looked at him and flashed a smile.

"I haven't treated you very good the last few years," Caleb said. "I haven't been a very good brother."

"Sometimes you make me feel unwanted," Connor said. "But most of the time I love being around you."

"I shouldn't ever make you feel unwanted. You are wanted. I'm just an ass sometimes, and I don't know why."

"We did a real-life treasure hunt together," Connor said, starting to get emotional. "We saved our sick mom. We escaped a forest fire and fought a wolf. You were with me the whole time, and I'm so glad that you were. I couldn't have done any of that without you."

"Yes, you could."

"Well, I wouldn't want to," said Connor. "I love you."

Caleb's eyes moistened and a wide smile spanned his face. He felt no need to counterbalance Connor's emotion this time. He felt the same way. "I love you, too." It felt weird to actually say it. But it felt good too. He put an arm around his brother.

They sat and watched the creek for a while, not feeling the need to say anything else.

Caleb had a warm, tingling feeling in his chest that spread throughout his body. He was happy they'd stayed back and had this conversation. He felt like he had formed the bond with his brother that should have always been there. He promised himself that he wouldn't let that bond slip away again.

His eyes drifted shut and his head fell forward. He awoke with a start and pulled his head back up. "Wow, I'm really tired."

"Me, too." Connor yawned.

They both lay back in the grass.

"You never told us what you would do if you had any extra money," Caleb said.

"That's easy," Connor said. "I'm gonna donate it to my burn camp."

"Oh yeah. That's awesome."

"It is," Connor said with a sleepy chuckle. "Let's take a nap."

"Yeah. Just a quick one though, we gotta go tell them about the treasure." Caleb couldn't believe that this perfect day still hadn't reached its climax. He couldn't wait to see the looks on their faces when they unzipped his backpack. He could picture it now.

Caleb thought he heard his brother say, "Now I lay me down to sleep," in a nearly inaudible whisper.

His eyes closed. Connor's words faded away as he began to dream. It was strange: he could feel himself dreaming. He was aware that he was still lying near the creek, but....

His feet felt warm in the sand. The waves crashed against the beach ahead of him. The ocean stretched out across the entire horizon. He looked down, and wasn't surprised to find that he was little again. As his feet began slapping on the darker, wet sand, he turned around and saw his family. Connor was running to catch up to him. Mom and Dad held hands and watched from further back. The water rushed in and covered his feet. Pure joy washed over him. The sea that had once seemed so ominous now beckoned him.

He dove into a waist-high wave. He wasn't afraid.

Epilogue

RAY WAS BORED. Everyone at his house was sleeping. Ara had returned with an unusual bounce in her step, then went directly to bed.

He decided that he'd go see if Connor and Caleb still wanted to play. He could also find out what their parents had said about the gold.

He grabbed a handful of pink- and white-frosted animal cookies and set off for their place. He kept his eyes focused on the trees, but he didn't feel that scared anymore. Connor had smacked that wolf good. He probably wouldn't ever want to come back.

When he arrived at the yard he saw Spencer and Amber lying in the grass under the enormous willow tree. They were sleeping, cuddled up in the spoon position.

He crept past them and knocked on the sliding glass door. No one answered. He pulled the handle and it slid open.

"Hello?" he said.

Nothing. The house was silent.

He walked in and tried the door to the nearest bedroom he saw. No one was there. He opened the door across the hall with the same results. He walked across the living room and opened another door. This room was bigger, so he went inside. There were two books laying on the nightstand. One of them was called *The Gold Rush of 1857,* the other was *The Gold Bug.* He'd never heard of The Gold Bug, but it sounded good. He flipped through it, found no pictures, and put it back on the nightstand.

He came back out in the living room. *Where are they? And why is everyone so sleepy?* He decided that they would probably be back any minute, so he'd wait for them here. He turned on a radio that was sitting on the kitchen counter.

"...spreading rapidly throughout the country. All people need to isolate——"

He turned the knob until he picked something else up.

"...*a mysterious marking that many are referring to as the angel kiss, usually on the forehead, indicates approximately twelve hours until the coma phase begins.*" He saw a Rubik's Cube sitting near the toaster. He picked it up and began spinning the colors around as the radio droned on in the background. "*The coma phase has been reported to last approximately three hours. During those hours, the patient cannot be woken. Then, they are overcome by—* "

He flipped the knob again, searching for music. The Rubik's cube was frustrating. The lack of music on the radio wasn't helping.

"...*genetic mutation of avian influenza, or bird flu, has devastated Europe with a nearly hundred percent mortality rate in humans, as well as all species of birds. Unfortunately, it is both the most contagious and deadliest virus the world has ever——*"

He turned the radio off, tossed the cube back on the counter, and went outside. He heard a faint meow coming from the general direction of the willow tree. He tiptoed past the sleeping grownups and under the tree. Its hanging branches brushed his cheeks as he passed through.

The meowing was getting louder. On the other side of the tree was a barely visible path. He followed it as it made a left turn and he came upon a wooden garden shed. The meows were coming from inside.

He tried the door, but it was locked with a combination padlock. The cat inside was scratching on the door.

He walked around the side of the shed and saw a small, cantilever window that was cracked open. The window was too high for him to reach.

He looked around and found a barrel around the back of the shed. There was nothing inside but some yard debris. He tipped the barrel over, rolled it under the window, and climbed up on it.

He looked inside and saw a gray cat with white paws. *It must be Connor's cat,* he thought. He'd heard Connor mention his cat, Punky, once or twice in the last few days.

He tilted open the window and called, "Here, kitty, kitty."

Punky jumped up on the workbench in the middle of the shed, knocking several pieces of pipe to the floor, and began meowing, loudly.

"Come on, Punky," Ray said. "You can do it."

She sprang across to the other workbench that sat under the window, this time knocking over two cans of gold spray paint as she leapt. A shiny gold cap popped off of one of the cans and spun around like a top. Ray was mesmerized by it for a moment.

Punky awkwardly climbed up a table-top saw and stretched her paws toward the window. Ray shook his head back into reality, then reached in the window and lifted her through it.

"Good kitty," he said as he stroked her fur. She purred and nuzzled Ray's chin.

He put her down and she strolled away into the woods with a smudge of gold paint on her tail.

Okay, those guys should be back by now, Ray thought. *Maybe I missed them out by the creek or something.*

He strolled up the trail to the creek humming to himself.

As he neared the creek, he caught a movement out of the corner of his eye. He turned his head and saw a big frog hopping toward the water. He bent down and caught it.

"Hey, froggy," he said. He absolutely loved frogs.

The frog looked at him and blinked. It was greenish brown and it had four dark spots on its back in the shape of a diamond.

This day just keeps getting better and better, he thought as he yawned.

He held the frog up to his face and smiled from ear to ear.

He imagined that the frog smiled back at him.

Acknowledgments

THANK YOU TO MY BROTHER: our adventures in the creek behind our apartment provided the original inspiration behind this story. Our bond has always meant the world to me, even though I often haven't shown it or deserved it.

To Mom, who has always put us before herself, and who is now the most treasured Nana in the world.

To Dad, who is my polar opposite in so many ways, but who I know would do anything for me.

To Rob, the best stepfather a kid could possibly hope for.

ACKNOWLEDGMENTS

To James Ford, simply a genuine friend. Everyone should have a dogg like him. His input, constructive criticism, and encouragement was invaluable during the writing process.

To Jordan Chaney, whose expertise, guidance, and friendship has been invaluable.

To all my other friends, who don't even know I wrote a book yet because I'm too self-conscious to admit it, but who have been an extremely important part of my life, too.

To my fire department family, for their integrity, loyalty, and self-sacrifice, not just in emergencies, but in everyday life. Mostly just thanks for the constant entertainment and laughs.

To my Eyabsut Family, whose strength, humor, and kindness in the face of adversity has uplifted me for years.

To my editor, Claire Allen, who went above and beyond in helping a clueless first-time author.

To Judith Briles and Bobby Crew at Author U: without you, this wouldn't be printed as an actual book right now.

To Larry Yoder, who helped me with the finishing touches.

To Gregory Hill, who took time from writing and rocking to read a stranger's manuscript and give lots of advice and encouragement.

To my sons, Kaden and Ashton. You bring brilliance and meaning to my life. You make every day an adventure. I love you more than words could ever say...

Go Hawks!

THANK YOU!!!

Author Biography

KYLE LOCKHAVEN lives with his wife, Alicia, and two sons in Washington state. They have an old dog named Wookie. His sons have an orange cat named Milo and a bearded dragon named Sandy. Kyle works as a firefighter/paramedic. This novel, his first, won the Draft to Dream book competition.

CPSIA information can be obtained
at www.ICGtesting.com
Printed in the USA
FFOW02n1142180718
47443277-50705FF